Also by Donal Ryan

The Spinning Heart
The Thing About December
A Slanting of the Sun: Stories

Praise for *All We Shall Know*

"A democratic work of genius. I was buckled by it, floored by it."
—Sebastian Barry, author of *Days without End*

"Donal Ryan's new book is an enthrallingly impassioned and compassionate read, ferocious but humane. *All We Shall Know* acknowledges the acts of vicious self-destruction the human heart is capable of but does not accept the irreparability of such acts. To his raw, wounded and grieving characters Donal Ryan says: If you are still breathing, you can be redeemed."
—Colin Barrett, author of *Young Skins*

"Stunning." —*The Bookseller* (London)

"I read it with enormous pleasure. He is a remarkably imaginative and beautiful user of the language. This book is very moving and true. I love the truth in his work."
—Jennifer Johnston, author of *Naming the Stars*

"All that we've come to expect from Donal: great humanity and an uncanny sense of place but this time—and at last!—we have a man writing from a woman's point of view in a totally convincing and non-patronising way."
—Christine Dwyer Hickey, author of *Last Train from Liguria*

"An extraordinary portrait of adultery, loneliness, and betrayal . . . One of the finest writers working in Ireland today . . . worthy of Greek drama . . . in the great tradition of tragic fiction, his lonely adulteress coming to grief in the same shadowy spaces as Emma Bovary or Anna Karenina." —John Burnside, *The Guardian* (London)

"A consummate artist . . . The denouement offers a satisfying element of redemption . . . a great writer whose steady maturation proceeds apace."   —*The Sunday Times* (London)

"Raw, radiant prose . . . [a] wonderful novel."
                                        —*Sunday Express* (London)

"[A] gem of a novel. With a sure sense of place, and a convincing portrayal of life lived at the edgy margins, it vividly plots the landscape of the heart en route to a gripping and ultimately redemptive finale."   —*Daily Mail* (London)

"Shines through its female characters."   —*Irish Tatler*

"A stunning story that deserves great success."
                                        —*Good Housekeeping*

"An intense, dramatic story . . . rather touching."
                                        —*The Mail on Sunday* (UK)

All We Shall Know

Donal Ryan

PENGUIN BOOKS

PENGUIN BOOKS

An imprint of Penguin Random House LLC
375 Hudson Street
New York, New York 10014
penguin.com

First published in Great Britain by Doubleday,
an imprint of Penguin Random House, 2016
Published in Penguin Books 2017

Library of Congress Cataloging-in-Publication Data

Names: Ryan, Donal, 1977– author.
Title: All we shall know / Donal Ryan.
Description: New York, New York : Penguin Books, 2017.
Identifiers: LCCN 2017007688 (print) | LCCN 2017011738 (ebook) |
ISBN 9781524704834 (ebook) | ISBN 9780143131045 (paperback)
Subjects: LCSH: Pregnancy—Fiction. | Teacher-student relationships—Fiction. |
Secrecy—Fiction. | BISAC: FICTION / Literary. | FICTION / Family Life. |
FICTION / Contemporary Women. | GSAFD: Domestic fiction
Classification: LCC PR6118.Y354 (ebook) | LCC PR6118.Y354 A79 2017 (print) |
DDC 823/.92—dc23
LC record available at https://lccn.loc.gov/2017007688

Printed in the United States of America
1   3   5   7   9   10   8   6   4   2

Set in Electra LH

For Anne Marie, with love

All We Shall Know

Week Twelve

MARTIN TOPPY IS the son of a famous Traveller and the father of my unborn child. He's seventeen, I'm thirty-three. I was his teacher. I'd have killed myself by now if I was brave enough. I don't think it would hurt the baby. His little heart would stop with mine. He wouldn't feel himself leaving one world of darkness for another, his spirit untangling itself from me.

At seven weeks or so a foetus starts to move. Imperceptibly, they say, but I swear I felt a stirring yesterday, a tiny shifting, a shadow-weight. I've been still and silent all these weeks, listening for him. I sit here with the curtains drawn and the TV muted, waiting for a hint of something in the soft glow of things detonating, people bleeding, corpses being carried swathed in flags by dark-eyed men, people arguing and kissing and driving in cars, people opening and closing their mouths.

I've measured his time from the actual minute, not from the

first day of my last period, like a doctor would, where a woman would be having normal sex, a normal life, and wouldn't know one moment from another. But all my moments now are marked and measured, standing out in unforgiving light to be examined.

Pat came back yesterday evening from weeks of work around the country, installing water meters. They had to stay in digs, he said; the work was round the clock. The day he left he bent and kissed me on the cheek. His lips were cold; he paused before he straightened. I can't remember if I looked at him. That was on the second day of the seventh week.

I stood at the TV-room door last night and looked at him, stretched along the couch in his tracksuit bottoms and Liverpool jersey, barefoot, unshaven, soft-bellied, defenceless. I'm pregnant, I said. He swung his head towards me and there was a sharp light in his eyes – was it maybe joy? – that extinguished itself after a moment, as he remembered. I told him the father was a man I'd met online, in the voice I always use to make him know I'm serious. Low and even.

He sat up, then stood before me and shouted, JESUS! just once. Then he raised his fists as though to punch me, but he pulled back and punched the air before my face instead, and he said, I'll kill you, I'll kill you, and he put his fists to his eyes and cried, very hard, teeth bared, eyes closed, like a little boy who's just felt shocking pain.

There wasn't much more to be said or done then, so he left. He was white as he walked with his gear-bag towards the front door, two small discs of livid red in the centres of his cheeks. He looked back at me from the open doorway. He was ghostly, washed in pale-orange light.

Are we even now? His voice was low, almost a whisper. I didn't reply.

I always loved you, Melody Shee, he said.

All I said back was, Goodbye, Pat.

I slept deeply last night, for a while at least. I didn't dream, or if I did I don't remember. My body has started to do its own thing, to do what needs to be done. I'm twelve weeks gone, and two days. I announced my pregnancy at the twelve-week mark, as is customary. At twelve weeks the immediate danger has passed, the child has learnt to be, to cling, to grow and grow. Around this time a baby starts to taste. I feel I should be spooning sugar down, to sweeten his world. I tried some ice cream earlier today but it felt too cold in my chest and too hot in my belly, and a few minutes later it came back up. I have a craving now for bacon, wrapped in white bread, with butter and ketchup. He prefers savoury, so.

Pat's father let himself in here sometime in the hour after dawn. I got up and walked around behind him, like a ghost he couldn't see. He took a bagful of clothes from the walk-in wardrobe he'd made for us himself as a first-anniversary gift. He took Pat's hurling helmet and togs and boots, and his laptop, and his pile of folders and papers from beside his desk in the small spare room. He left the front door open to ease his quarrying, armful by armful, of his son's life. He forgot the power supply for Pat's laptop, so I unplugged it and wound it neatly and handed it to him. He looked at me for the first time. His face was red with anger and embarrassment, and his breathing was heavy and ragged. I wanted to make him a cup of tea and rub his arm and tell him not to worry, and hear him calling me *love* and *sweetheart*, and see him smiling fondly at me, the way he always used to.

I'm sorry, Paddy, I said. I could almost feel his palpitating heart, rippling the air between us. I wanted to tell him to go easy, to mind his poor heart.

Ah, look, he said. Look. And he had no more words for me, nor I for him.

His car was backed into the yard, boot open, engine running. Fumes curled inwards along the hall. I thought, That would be a way to do it. He drove out and stopped on the avenue and walked back to close the gate. Like a protective grandfather, like a man who might say: Better keep that oul gate shut, for fear at all the child might run out in front of a car.

Yesterday's ripple of sickness is a great wave today, rolling in and crashing over me every few minutes. A terrible tiredness came on me this morning and I sat on the couch for most of the day, with a basin at my feet. I rinse it out every now and then, in the kitchen sink. My muscles ache each time I walk, and my head spins when I get up and when I sit down, and pins and needles prick my goosebumped skin. I don't remember eating, but I must have, because there are crumbs on the kitchen counter, and the rind of an orange.

Morning sickness my arse. The vomiting subsides in the early evening. I slept last night in my dressing-gown, cocooned in doubled-over duvets. The air in our room is always cold, except for a few weeks in midsummer. Pat always loved the coldness of the air: he said it made the bed more cosy to have a bit of yourself cold, your toes or the top of your head; you could appreciate being in bed a lot more. Oh, Pat. All the fights fought and terrible words spoken, all the years of nicks and cuts and scattered days when we tore each other so vicious and so deep. And this is what I've done to end it. Announced from the TV-room door that I'd let another man do what you couldn't. I've been on my hands and knees for numberless hours. This is more than I can bear and less than I deserve. We'll slip away to darkness soon enough, and live inside it, just us two, once I have all my loose ends neatly tied.

*

This morning I stood barefoot on the decking, drinking tea. The sickness was gone. I thought about having a fag. My body felt neutral, except for a twitch now and then from the muscles in my abdomen, as though aimless electrons were pulsing along it, shot from some confused gland that had been sleeping up to now. The air was clear and clean and there was a faint smell of mown grass. Someone nearby doing their first cut. I looked at the clay flower-pot at the far corner of the decking that Pat used for years as a giant ashtray, without ever thinking to empty it, overflowing with butts and black muck. My stomach churned a little bit.

I imagined the decking to be a gallows, the wooden planks beneath my feet its trapdoor. An audience of thistles and tufts of grass. I touched the belt of my dressing-gown. I thought of the high hook on the bathroom wall. I wondered how long it would take and how much it would hurt. I wondered if there were Stanley blades in Pat's virgin toolbox in the cracked, untreated shed. I thought about a deep bath of roasting water. Why does the bathroom seem to be the natural place? The water and soap and disinfectant, the white tiles on the floor and walls, easily cleaned, the clouding steam. There's something attractive about the dark inversion of leaving the world and curling myself into a cramped, warm space.

I ate: a boiled egg and dry toast. It stayed down. I slept.

Week Thirteen

MY DAYS ARE quadranted neatly now. I wake promptly at eight as I always have. I spend the first hour of each day convinced that I will actually kill myself. I feel relieved. I spend the hour after that worrying about the consequences of killing myself. My relief evaporates. I spend the next hour convinced that I will not kill myself. I feel relieved again. I spend the hour after that worrying about the consequences of not killing myself. My relief evaporates. I repeat this cycle three more times and I go to bed. I sleep for eight hours.

What thread has me tethered to this earth? Fear of pain. And a picture in my head of my father's panicked eyes, having seen the squad car draw up outside with Father Cotter in the passenger seat. His hands shaking as he fumbles with the lock, reaching for the jamb to hold himself upright. His legs buckling in a weakness, big Jim Gildea stepping forward, kind, strong, embarrassed, or a young guard, red-faced and awkward, desperate for their ordeal to be over, catching a hold of him and helping him inside to a chair. A picture in my head of him standing alone at my grave, a cold wind on his face, a look of incomprehension in his eyes, his embarrassment as he accepts the sympathy of friends and barely remembered acquaintances with words that don't sound right in his ears: Thanks; You're very good to come; At least the rain held off; She's in a better place; She's with her mother now. The thought of his aloneness, the completeness of his sorrow, the idea of his world containing nothing, only sadness.

I dreamt last night, one of those dreams that seem so vivid you wake and lie in bed and wonder for a while what's real. I was in a meeting of the Kurt Cobain Club. Breedie Flynn was sitting cross-legged and barefoot in her shorts and I was sitting cross-legged in front of her, watching her. Streams of tears flowed along her cheeks, pooling for moments in tiny valleys formed by acne before falling floorwards. Breedie's face was livid and pitted; Breedie's face was so beautiful I sometimes hated her. We were in Breedie's bedroom in my dream, and we had tented a sheet above our heads between a chair-back and Breedie's bed, and we had sandbagged ourselves against the world with pillows and cushions and Breedie's collection of stuffed animals from her childhood.

   Breedie Flynn and I founded the Kurt Cobain Club in April of 1994. Breedie thought he was a god; I just thought he was gorgeous. Kurt Cobain had chronic stomach pain all of his short life. So did my beautiful friend Breedie. She spoke to a poster of him as though he was in the room; I listened embarrassed and I never looked in her face when she almost absent-mindedly held my hand. I liked when she did, though. The Kurt Cobain Club owned these things: a Ouija board we would use to try to summon the spirit of Kurt Cobain; a litre bottle of vodka we would drink from in terrified sips; a tape recorder and microphone we would use to make recordings of Breedie Flynn's wild stories and imagined conversations in the perfectly mimicked voices of the cool girls, the fellas, the teachers, our parents, with a backing track of my screams of laughter.

Breedie looked at me in my dream and said, Melody, why did you leave me? And she reached for my hand and squeezed it and she was haloed by a blazing light and her hand was burning hot and I woke then, saying, *Breedie, oh, Breedie, I'm sorry*, and lay sweating in the cold air, and felt the creeping nausea hasten to a rush.

My father rings me every day to tell me things he thinks that I should know.

He was out at the bottle bank earlier. Someone had thrown a load of rubbish into it. He said, Lord, isn't it a fright? The CCTV cameras were broken, of course. I tut into a gap of silence and he goes on: I met Mossy Shanley yesterday evening below in the hurling field. The minors lost to Kildangan. Mossy hadn't a good word for poor old Jack Matt-And. He called him every name you could think of and a few you'd never think of. You'll have no luck, I told him, speaking ill of the dead like that. Eff that, says he, and he spat on the ground. Just because he's dead it doesn't mean he wasn't a bollix. Mossy said that, imagine. Lord, poor Jack. He hadn't a bad bone. All he ever wanted was to have a drink and to tell a story. I saw a lad earlier when I was walking home from devotions, and he driving along and he holding his telephone to his ear with one hand and he fixing his hair with the other hand and no hand at all on the steering wheel. Maybe it's a thing that he had a third hand sprouting from somewhere but if he had I couldn't see it. I could not.

And he stops and he waits for me to say something back, and he listens for sadness in my voice, I know. Will you call over this way one of the days?

I will, Dad.

I know you're busy giving the reading and writing lessons and all.

I am a bit all right, Dad.

Is it the same little tinker lad you do have all the time?

Traveller, Dad.

Oh, ya, Traveller. Lord, everyone is gone fierce particular about what they're called these days.

I'll have to leave the house soon. Time passes as a crawling on my skin, from my scalp to my soles and back up again. I'll have to get food, to stay alive while I'm waiting to die, and something for this sickness. Start of second trimester: morning sickness ends. I read that in a book, put just like that, set out perfunctorily as a fact, unassailable, incontrovertible, beneath a photo of a beautiful, smiling, perfect mother-to-be. What if your fucking morning sickness only started at the end of the first trimester? I'd nearly swallow a fistful of Valiums now, just to lie becalmed awhile, and drift away. There's a full bottle on the medicine shelf in the bathroom press. There's vodka in the cocktail cabinet and tonic in the fridge and ice in the freezer. Jesus, the party I could have. Will we do it, little man? I don't know why I'm so sure it's a boy. I just think of the child as the father compressed: red-cheeked and blue-eyed and dark-haired and beautiful. If I'm still alive when this tide of sickness turns I'll go and visit my father.

So here I am still, less sick but no more mobile. Aren't I rightly landed? Forty years ago I'd have been taken bodily away and set to work on the stained vestments of righteous men, the shirts and smocks and socks and smalls of those still in good standing with the Almighty, my baby dragged from me and sold and spirited away to live in grace away from my foulness. I feel a burden of freedom, a cloying sense of open space; I've been sitting now for hours on end unable to rise or to leave this room because I can't think which direction I would turn at the door: away down the hall to bed, or out the door to my car? Where would I go? I have enough money to do me a year or maybe more, and this quietness I longed for soon will pass, and everything I wished would end will come crashing to a start again: Pat will bang against the door and beg, and try to make me say I only lied, and I'll open it to the length of the chain and he'll reach through the gap towards me and cry and say, Please, Melody, please. I need you, Melody. Because he always needed me, and still to this day I can't think why.

I could still fly to London and end this, and come back and say, Yes, Pat, I was lying, and he could persuade himself to believe me, and we could take a weekend break somewhere and be massaged together, and walk along a river hand in hand, and stand beneath a waterfall and feel the spray on our faces and laugh, and think about the cave behind the falling water, cut off from the world, and all the roaring peace to be found there, and have a drink in the bar after dinner, and go to bed, and turn to one another's flesh for warmth, and find only a hard coldness there, and no accommodation, no forgiveness of sins; and we'd turn away again from one another, and lie apart facing upwards and send words into eternity about babies never born, and needs unmet, and prostitutes and internet sex and terrible unforgivable sins and swirling infinities of blame and hollow retribution, and we could slow to a stop as the sun crept up, and turn from each other in familiar exhaustion, and sleep until checking-out time on pillows stained with tears.

Thoughts sharpen themselves on the flints of one another and pierce me like a knife in my middle, sunk deep and twisted around. How we couldn't make ourselves remember, Pat and me. How we loved one other. If only we could have been perfectly dispassionate a moment, viewers from outside, or above, had out-of-body experiences, like floating spirits unshackled from their slashed-open, heart-stopped bodies in a blood-soaked surgery, watching their own evisceration without feeling the pain of it.

He fairly crippled himself, my Pat, with the weight of the expectations of others: his mother, his father, his sister, his friends, his monomaniacal hurling trainers, me. He told me once, not so many years ago, when we were still capable of reason, that he'd never once felt small until he'd met big men. He laughed but he wasn't joking. I watched the tears lay siege behind his eyes. My heart tore for him; it physically pained me. I had no other words, I could only whisper that I loved him, there was that, there'd always be that. And still, even after that, knowing what I knew, having said what I'd said, having wanted so badly to take his pain from him and make it my own, I started only short years later to give my days to making him feel smaller. I waged war against him, and he waged war on me.

You have a fine fat arse for a one that's forever on a diet, he would tell me.

You're like a simple child that's only barely toilet-trained, I would tell him, the amount of piss you get on the floor.

He'd say: A lot you'd know about children, simple or otherwise.

I'd say: You must have a fair shitty seed the way it won't take properly.

He'd say: Why don't you write a poem about it? And send it in to the paper? The way the neighbours can all have a good laugh again. Give the lads below in Ciss's a good howl. Do you know they all read your poems out to each other down there and piss themselves laughing?

I'd tell him he was no man, he was never a man.

He'd tell me I must have a cold cunt of a womb to say no child would stay in it.

I'd call him rotten, and disgusting, and a pervert, and a prick, and I'd roar my throat raw. I'd tell him that I'd never loved him.

He'd tell me in a flat, steady voice that he hated my guts.

How did we turn to such savagery? How did love's memory fade so completely from us? The things we said, the things we thought. My poor Pat, my lovely man, my twinkling boy, my hero. Oh, me, oh, cruel, cruel me, I never knew myself. Tomorrow, I'll have forgotten myself again.

Week Fourteen

I FELL IN love with Pat the day I first saw him play hurling. He was sent off that day, and he looked at me as he walked from the field, and he pointed at me as if to say, That was for you, and the lad he'd punched was still on the ground, and little skirmishes were erupting around the ref and the fallen player, a fella I'd slow-danced with months before at a Foróige disco, who'd ignored me afterwards and shifted someone on the way home in the bus, and had said something smart about me in school on the Monday but I don't know to this day what, and Pat took off his helmet as he walked with one sweeping movement and his hair was wet with sweat and swept back from his forehead and the sun lit his face and his blue eyes blazed and they held mine and he pointed to his heart as he strode through the cool evening air towards the sideline and my legs felt so weak I thought I'd fall down on the ground, and Breedie Flynn was saying, Oh, my God, Melody, he's pointing at *you*, and she was squeezing my arm, and oh, sweet Jesus, how I loved him, loved him, loved him.

Pat was the first boy I ever kissed, whose hand I ever held, and was, until thirteen and a bit weeks ago, the only boy I'd ever kissed. I'd never felt another man's hand on my cheek, or seen that piercing light of longing in another man's eyes. We merged over time into one person, I think, and it's easy to be cruel to oneself. I can only now separate myself from him, now that we're properly separate. Even through the hating years we were always close by each other.

I felt like I was doing it wrong, the first time we kissed. Breedie Flynn and I had practised on each other, but we'd never used our tongues, reasoning that to do so would make us lezzers, and anyway we laughed too much to get any serious research done. Breedie drew back from me once and put her hand on my cheek and I put my hand on top of hers and we looked into each other's eyes and time moved liquidly to a forking of paths, and then I laughed and so did she, just at the point of divergence. The universe makes and remakes itself in each moment. I feel those other lives sometimes, going on around me.

Pat seemed like a really good kisser. He never bit into my lip the way I'd heard some girls say their fellas did, or squeezed my nipples, or tried too roughly to get his hand up my skirt or down my pants. I felt embarrassed at first, unsure what to do, but soon kissing Pat was the most right thing in the world, a thing I just did, like singing in my head as I walked, or looking at the sky's different blues, or listening in the night to the whispering breeze and hearing my mother's voice.

My mother and father didn't fit together. She was taller than him by an inch or so; she had long slender hands and his were thick and stub-fingered. She was an aesthete and a classicist; he didn't know what these things were. She wanted to work as an academic, but she never did. He worked as a foreman for the council, on the roads mostly. My mother always smelt of French perfume and expensive leather; my father always seemed to smell of sweat, and something sharp and heavy, bitumen maybe, or whatever dark and tarry things filled his days. My father didn't seem to interest her, or to excite her. He didn't make her weary, the way another man might have, a man more able to read her silences, to decipher the algorithms of her. That's what she saw in him, I think.

You should be a manager by now, I heard her tell him one morning.

I'm not equipped for that sort of a job, he said.

I heard her sniff, and I heard a long silence, and I heard a chair being pulled out from the table, and I heard my father say, Right, well, in his soft voice, and I heard him picking up his keys, and then I heard her say: What *are* you equipped for? What *are* you equipped for? What are you good for? What *good* are you, Michael?

And I heard my father say, I don't know. Sure, look, I'll see you later. And he left through the back door, and he didn't even slam it, and there was no sound of movement from the kitchen, but I could smell cigarette smoke, and the air felt cold around me in the hallway where I stood listening.

My father seemed different to me when he came home that evening. I was barely ten, and I'd only ever thought of him in terms of love. Some childish opacity had fallen away; the suffusing light that had always in my vision surrounded him was dimmed, flickering towards extinction. I appraised him, coldly. What was he good for?

Thinking now about the way I thought about things then, about how I let my mother's anger towards him seep into me, I feel a desperate need to apologize, to mitigate the hurt I must

have caused him as I drew away from him, as I let my perfect love
for him be sullied, and eroded, and disintegrated, by the coldness
of a woman I didn't even really like, but whom I wanted more
than anything to be like.

I didn't run into his arms that evening, so he knew that something had changed; I walked to meet him at the door, and there
was a stiffness and an awkwardness between us, and he must have
sensed that I was suddenly no longer a child, but another woman
in his house, an addition to, an extension of, the woman already
there, who seemed to need him and who seemed to despise him,
and sometimes, often, to hate him.

He was shocked at the change in me, but he didn't let on. I
knew by the way he was looking at me with his eyebrows closing
together, holding me from him at arm's length by the shoulders,
seeing whatever hard light he saw every day in my mother's eyes,
and laughing, as though he couldn't believe it, but should have
known all along that this would happen. I think he started that
day, at that moment of strangeness between us, on his journey to
being a duffer, a run-of-the-mill old man, a quiet, boring person,
who just existed, moving through his days out of duty, a sense of
having to see this thing through, this raising of a child and sup-
porting of a wife, this series of payments that had to be met, with
nothing to grasp at the end of it all, no soft bed of thanks to lie
upon, no sweet relief that his work was done, and done well, and
those he worked for were grateful, and loving, and adoring.

But still he loved me, defiantly, fiercely, and he loved her the
same way, because what else was there for him to do?

I was fourteen the first time I lost my reason. It was the sight of my
mother's fingers that ignited me. The way they had been arranged,
unnaturally, with a rosary beads artfully twined into them. I
somehow had failed to notice it, or I had seen it but the seeing

hadn't landed on me. Our family doctor had given me an injection of something the night before to help me sleep, to take me away from the pain. We were standing at our chief mourners' posts, Daddy and me, Mercury and Venus at our extinguished Sun, Mammy's brothers and sisters arranged to our sides like the farther-out planets, an asteroid belt of cousins near the doors, lined along the vestibule.

I said, Daddy, what the *fuck* are those rosary beads doing there? She never said the rosary in her *life*. Daddy didn't look at me. He swallowed hard; something in his throat clicked. I remember the paleness of him, his gritted teeth, the tiny tremor in his head that only I could see as I stood incandescent beside him.

It's okay, pet, he whispered. It's always done that way; they just presumed.

Presumed? I nearly screamed, and I saw through the arched door at the far end of the parlour a cousin, barely more than an infant, giggling in the vestibule. I broke from our small rank of chief mourners and pushed through the stream of duty-doers towards the daylight. Chief mourners, intermediate mourners, minor mourners, all staring at me, their eyes following me out; a bit of fun suddenly, out of the blue, a breaking light in the sombre day. I rushed at him and he never saw me coming, or if he did he didn't know it was for him I was coming, and I smacked the giggling cousin across the side of his head. My hand made a sound like a whip-crack on his skull. He'd only have been eight, nine at the most. Then I whirled away from him and grabbed Frank Doorley's meaty arm. He'd been standing sentry at the entrance, guarding the hospice donation box. Get in there and take those beads from my mother's hands. He didn't move. Get. The fuck. In there. NOW.

And so, at a weary nod from my father, he did. And the

entrance door had to be closed for a few minutes, and my little
cousin, who had hardly known my mother, contorted his face in
a keening, breathless cry and was hugged and shushed kindly by
older children and whisked away, and the truncated line of neighbours and friends and my father's workmates and half-remembered
relatives shook the offered hands and filed away from the
embarrassment of it all in grave procession, and Daddy stood still
and white and watched while Frank Doorley prised and teased
and finally cut the offending beads from Mammy's translucent
hands.

Do you, Melody, take this man, to have and to hold, to love,
honour and obey, to fight with on the way to the hotel over the
rusty heap of shit of a wedding car his cousin turned up with after
promising a nearly new Mercedes, to pinch so hard through the
sleeve of his shirt while the photos are being taken under the
willow tree by the lake that his eyes fill with tears, to not let even
the sight of those tears soften your rage, to not give him one kind
word all day, to make it pure obvious to the whole top table that
you're like a lunatic with him, to see the familiar worry and
sadness and miserable resignation in your father's eyes, to come
round a bit after a few glasses of Prosecco, to fall back into it after
he leaves you for nearly half an hour to smoke fags with his idiot
friends out the back, to lift your dress in the vestibule where
nobody could see and kick him on the shin so hard he goes white,
to tell him during the first dance that you knew all along he'd
ruin the whole day, to turn your arse to him in your first connubial
bed, to fight with him every day of the fortnight in the Canaries,
to look up at him one day from a bed in the Regional Hospital
and tell him he didn't care, you knew well he didn't, that he'd
never wanted a baby, that he was probably delighted, that it
wouldn't have suited him one bit, that he'd never have been able

for the responsibility, that at least now his time with the lads wouldn't be affected, to open the boot of his car a week later and find a carrier bag full of baby clothes, and a little Liverpool jersey, with SHEE written along the back of it, for richer or poorer, in sickness and in health, until death do you part?

The sky has been a heavy grey for days. I've been lying down a long time. The air in here is warm and dank, bitter in my mouth. My thoughts come in fast and move away from me before I can grasp one and focus on it, as though they've been fashioned into a string that's being fed into and pulled through my conscious-ness. My head is heavy. The lip of the couch cushion is a precipice: if I rolled I'd fall and fall. The doorbell rang an hour ago, or maybe it was a day. My phone's been buzzing on the coffee-table but I can't reach that far across. I feel I might die of this sickness. I hope I do, just die here on this couch. I can't lift my hand against myself; I can barely lift my hand at all. Was I born without courage? If I could just give up my ghost I would. There'd be a post-mortem, and an inquest, but it would all be routine, done to satisfy obligations. It was natural causes, just one of those things, mapped by Fate's unknowable hand. She was pregnant, tragically, when the fatal arrhythmia struck. And only Pat would know the truth.

　　Tomorrow if I'm able I'll raise myself, and get a glass of milk from the kitchen, and a packet of biscuits. And I'll open the win-dow a little, to change the air in here. And then I'll shower and dress myself, and get into my car and go to the halting site where Martin Toppy lives, and I'll give him back his worn and dog-eared copy of the only book we ever read together that had more pages of words than pictures, because it seems important somehow that I do, and I'll apologize to him if I can, and then I'll go to the house I grew up in and I'll sit at my father's table, and be kind to

him, and let him be kind to me, and make him know somehow
he's not to blame. And then I'll take my courage and my leave of
all these troubles. The vodka and the Valium, I think.

I left the house today on wobbly legs and walked around the block
to get my blood flowing. Then I drove to the entrance of the estate
and stopped there and thought about turning back until a car
stopped behind me and forced me to move, and I drove out over
the Long Hill and down to the end of the Ashdown Road, and
turned left through an opening in a high wall, into a chaotic
aggregation of vans and caravans and tiny bungalows, all hidden
from the sight of settled eyes by a contrived dip, a municipally
mandated lowering of the ground, and a screen of concrete. I
asked a large man in brown pants and a string vest that half
covered an enormous stomach, who seemed to be some kind of a
sentry, where the Toppys lived. He regarded me blank-faced from
his mucky post, before moving slowly towards me and bending a
bit to better direct himself in my open window, and saying
wheezily, with a quizzical inflection: Haranoonah, noonah, wha?
He rested a stout bare arm on the roof of my car and waited
patiently for my answer to what was apparently his counter-
question.

From my right, the voice of a girl said: There's no point in
axing him nothing, miss.

The sentry made a querulous noise and he peeled himself
back to reveal, standing in the doorway of a small caravan
appended to a large mobile home, a small, pretty young woman
with a strawberry-blonde braid and skintight, stonewashed jeans.
There was a wooden trellis around her doorway. If spring was
farther along she'd have been framed by flowers. She said: Them
Toppys is all gone away. Do you want me to give them a message?
She walked down from the caravan door, descending the steps

and crossing the muck with a sway to her hips that was almost hypnotic.

I felt an unexpected sadness and an unexpected relief at this news. What would I have said, after all? How would I have met his eye? Why was I even there? I gave her Martin Toppy's book through my car window. They'll be back, she said, in summer sometime, or autumn. They're gone tarmacking, she said. Actually, she said *tarmacaddanin*. She looked at the book and I looked at her, standing beside my car, and the sentry looked at us both. There was a boldness about her, and a childish abruptness to her manner, and there was something else about her, I'm not sure what, that's made me think about her constantly since.

Which of the Toppys is it belonging to?

Martin, I told her.

And she said, There's a millen and wan Toppys in it. Big Martin, Small Martin or Old Martin? And I said I wasn't sure, and she said, You'd be sure if you'd ever laid eyes on Big Martin because he's massive so he is, and it's hardly belonging to Old Martin, so it must of been Small Martin. What's it about? she asked.

It's called *Danny, Champion of the World*, I said.

I can see what's it called, she said. I axed what's it about. She didn't look at me, just examined the cover of the book.

I was surprised, and riled a bit by her, and felt a distant longing as I looked at her, to be as young as her, and pretty, and self-possessed, and free. I told her it was about a boy who lived in a gypsy wagon with his father. They have great adventures together, I said. It's a story about childhood, and wonder, and the love between a father and a son.

That'd be right up Martin Toppy's alley, all right, the girl said. He's pure stone mad about his father. Mick Toppy is his father, you know. The only one of them not called Martin. Your Martin is his only boy. He'd of been a she-mickey only for him. Do you know what that is? A man that has bad seed only good for making girls. How's it these in the book lives in a gypsy wagon? Is it a wagon like mine or one of them old-fashioned ones that's pulled by horses? Are they gypsies in the book? You can't trust them people, you know. They'd steal the tooth from your mouth. How comes you have a book belonging to the Toppys?

And I told her I'd been helping Martin with his schoolwork. And she asked, What happened you that you're so sad? And I was silent in my shock and she was silent too, and she looked at me through eyes I've seen before, and I thanked her for taking charge of the book, and she promised to keep it safe until the Toppys returned, and as I tried to three-point turn my Fiesta on the muddy avenue with the aid of the wild-armed, indecipherably articulated directions of the sentry, she walked back up the steps to the door of her caravan, her wagon as she called it, and turned there and looked again at me, cradling Martin Toppy's book, and I saw the cheeky, playful expression on her lovely freckled face flit away, changing to something guarded, closed, defiant. And I looked at her again in my rear-view mirror from the entrance as I waited to pull out and she was standing there still, looking back at me, and sunlight danced around her in the window-glass and on her hair, and something in my heart was lifted, and I felt the baby settling down to sleep.

Week Fifteen

BREEDIE FLYNN IN geography. Across the room from me because we'd been separated for talking. Scowling at the cool girls in their huddled, smirking group. Curling her lip at the lads at the back, flicking a spit ball from her desk back towards them. They're talking too, sir, she suddenly says, and Hornycords Hannigan turns around from the blackboard, from his chalk diagram of the layers of the earth, and Breedie is pointing at the cool girls.

Worry about yourself, Miss Flynn, and the F you're going to get from me at Christmas.

You're going to give me an *F* for Christmas? An *eff*? And she draws the F along her breath and purses her lips to the shape of a kiss. And the lads laugh and the cool girls roll their eyes.

Hornycords takes his position facing us, sitting back against the edge of his desk. He seems priapic, as he always did, because of the way his perpetual corduroy trousers bunch at the fly. He folds his arms and opens his mouth to speak but Breedie gets there first.

I like your big erection, sir. And Hornycords Hannigan's eyes widen and swing towards her and his arms uncross and his hands swing down to form a shield across his crotch, of their own accord it seems, and he straightens himself and he opens his mouth but no sound comes out, and Breedie says, At the side of your house. Is it a kitchen extension or an extra bedroom?

And Hornycords flops empurpled into his chair and even the cool girls are laughing and Breedie Flynn winks across at me, and I wake up laughing and crying and I'm still here and she's long gone.

Dying seems as unreasonable as living. If only there could be a switch, a painless, instant shutting down, a certainty of stopping in the space between heartbeats. An assurance that no cells would burst, no vessels implode for want of air, no searing agonies would see us out, no ground or breaking waves would rush to meet us as we fell, and receive our bodies, broken and living still, aware of the receding light. I feel my baby's stillness, like he's hiding from my thoughts. Emotions travel through placentas; I read that in the book. My baby's tides turn at the pull of my gravity.

I studied English and history at the University of Limerick. I did a master's in journalism. I tried and tried: I wrote pieces about GM food and whaling and direct provision for asylum seekers; I reviewed books and films and plays; I wrote a searing article on inverted sexism as a trope in advertising. It was published in a broadsheet supplement, and when I looked at the online edition there was a stream of comments beneath it and my stomach burnt with the excitement of it all and I waded into them and saw myself being attacked and I mounted a defence of my position and I gloried in my new-found notoriety and I railed against this narrow, straitened, un-nuanced, reactionary brand of feminism, and declared myself to be a proponent of the purest form of equality, and I was so happy with myself, and I was never asked to write for that paper again.

I couldn't get regular work. I could sense Pat's delight. He desperately wanted to keep me, in every sense. I registered for substitute teaching work. I got none. I advertised grinds in English. No one wanted them – except, years later, Martin Toppy, and he didn't really: his father had misread my ad. They pulled up on the kerb outside in a blacked-out SUV. Will you taych that boy to read? Martin Toppy's father said. All he brang home from school was nits. The blessings of God on you. His face was dark, flat-nosed, battle-scarred. He was a bare-knuckle boxer who'd retired undefeated. There was talk around the town of drugs, protection rackets, laundered fuel. He had a faded ad, written in marker, in his hand. My mobile number and address were on it. I'd pinned it years before on the noticeboard in the church.

He handed me an envelope stuffed with cash and drove away and left his son standing outside my house, looking down at his feet, silent and dark-haired and sad.

I haven't gone to see my father yet. It seems less urgent now, since meeting that Traveller girl, and I can find no earthly connection between these things. Tomorrow, maybe. My father will be giving his days to standing at his sitting-room window, watching out for me. He'll have chocolate-chip cookies in the cupboard because he knows I like them. He'll have proper coffee, and he'll have the biscuits and the coffee arranged at either side of the French press he bought in Aldi, even though he has no idea how it works. He got it just for me because he knows I like that oul complicated coffee. I think of him standing in a supermarket aisle, picking

French presses up and examining them and putting them down again, trying to work out the differences between them, worrying he's getting the wrong one, asking the checkout assistant if he has the right sort of coffee bought to go with the yoke.

Thinking about my father makes my head reel. I just won't. I won't think about him. But I'll go tomorrow to see him for sure. I'll tell him I'm fine, and Pat is flat out, and I've been doing a few bits for magazines, and I'll bring them up to show him when they're out, and he'll say, Oh, God, do, be sure and do. I'd love to see them. He read an article I wrote for a Sunday paper once about abortion and I saw him redden and take his glasses off and wipe them and put them back on, over and over again, as though the reading of my article was hurting his eyes and he needed to stop every now and then, and I heard him say, Hmm, as he read, and he folded the paper to quarters after he'd finished, and he looked at me and said, Well done, love, that's very good, and he went an hour early to devotions.

I felt an urge today to fortify myself. I drove to town this morning and I bought folic-acid supplements and iron tablets. I asked the girl behind the counter for advice on what was safe to take in pregnancy. Her voice was soft and soothing but I couldn't hear her words: my eyes and mind were drawn to people at the other tills, people holding children by the hands, harried and happy, suffused with normality.

The little bottles are arranged on the kitchen table in front of my laptop. As I write, the table jiggles on its uneven legs. The bottles dance a little, like small children saying, Me, me, look at me. I asked Pat a million times to fix this table. I feel a spark of annoyance that could flame easily to anger. Imagine, I still have some left for him, after everything. I have to try to concentrate on breathing in and out, slowly, centring myself. Tapping these keys and watching these words form into sentences soothes me. I'll have to remember to delete all this.

Martin Toppy sat here in this seat for all of his lessons, and I sat across from him with my back to the window, facing away from the light. Pat always left as he arrived, and went to training or the clubhouse or a meeting of some parish thing or hurling thing or any of those things I'd stopped being interested in years ago, and they barely nodded if they passed each other in the kitchen or the hall. He spoke always in a whisper. His skin was dark and his hair was thick and black so that his eyes seemed even lighter in contrast, soft and baby-blue. His eyes seemed always to swim with sorrow; he seemed always on the very verge of tears. His first lesson with me was a year ago, or just over it. He barely spoke in those first two hours. He sat at my kitchen table with a mug of tea and a plate of chocolate biscuits untouched before him. His eyes were cast down, his cheeks were a livid red, even against his sun-browned skin. His hands were clasped together in his lap, prayer-like in mortification. I asked him if he knew the alphabet. He shook his head without looking up. I had no beginner material. I hadn't expected to be teaching literacy. My material was on the Shakespeare plays prescribed for the junior and senior cycles, on John B. Keane and Sean O'Casey and Kavanagh and Yeats, the modern novels and essay writing. But the notes felt crisp and fresh through the oil-stained envelope, and I thought, How hard can it be? I wrote out an upper- and lower-case alphabet on a sheet of poster paper with a thick black marker. His eyes followed my hand. I called it out to him, slowly. He nodded slightly as I sounded each letter. I wrote his name for him. Do you recognize it?

He shook his head. The tears were visible now in his eyes. He drew a big hand across them. I'm thick, he whispered. I'm thick, miss.

*

This baby is going nowhere. It's funny how I know. If I don't eat, it'll take what it needs from my blood and softening flesh. I knew from before the sickness, before the first crampless day, from the moment I let what happened happen, from the feeling of something fulfilling itself, some implacable notion of Fate. My first and second miscarriages happened at night; both times I was woken from dreams of my mother by a searing, stabbing pain, and found myself soaked in thick, dark wetness. The memories of the dreams came to me days later, and then only the impressions of them: my mother smiling at me, as she almost never did in life, and pressing her cold hand softly against my cheek, and saying, Don't worry, my love, don't worry.

Pat rang my mobile yesterday, late in the evening. What could he have to say to me? I let it ring out and he didn't leave a message or try again.

Week Sixteen

I DROVE BACK to the Ashdown Road today, and slowed to a near stop at the entrance to the halting site, and looked in along the muddy avenue, and saw only a child and a dog, and a pony tethered to a fence, and the child stood still and watched me until I drove away again. I don't remember any single thing occurring to me to prompt me to drive to that place. Some unknowable longing came over me that I felt could be assuaged only by going there. Some thought of there being a way to be found there to move around this impasse, to see clearly what needs to be done, what needs to become of me. A tinkers' camp, an alien place, full of things and people inscrutable to me, might offer up some insight, some clear vision, some relief from this graceless state. The sound of that girl's voice is in my head still, the vision of the boldness in her eyes, as bright and clear as the sadness in Martin Toppy's eyes. What am I looking for?

There's some irreparable fault in me. There's something

broken inside my head that stops me being normal. What normal person would do what I've done, would think what I've thought? I told Martin Toppy that evening as he dressed himself that I was sorry, and that he had to leave, and that he couldn't ever come back, and he turned to look at me from the doorway and said, I love you, miss, I'd kill any man for you. And I laughed at this sudden proclamation, this small exposition of his life outside my house, of the form he took outside of the two hours he spent on Wednesday evenings, reading children's books at my kitchen table, hunched and red-faced, smiling up at me now and then to receive his praise for a sentence completed without my help. Maybe he was heartened by my laugh, or felt there was some invite in it, some equivocation, and he said, Please, miss, don't banish me. And I laughed again, at the word he used, the old-fashioned sound of it, and put my hand over my face, and stood in the hallway crying a minute, and he didn't move, only stayed turned towards me in the doorway, with the light of the evening sun angled across his beautiful face, glinting in his blue eyes, splitting to its spectrum in his tears.

There were moments where Pat and I stopped at each other and talked reasonably about the madness. Times of quietness and drawn breaths, where the shelling rang in our heads but the earth around our battlefield was still, and we could see the sky and the circling birds, and sit for a while, weary and hollowed, and put terms on a temporary truce. We got together too young, we'd agree. If we'd gotten together in our twenties it would all have been fine. We should have seen more of the world, and less of each other, and more of other people. We fastened ourselves too tightly together; we were two people sharing one life, so we had only half a life each. We hadn't been fair to each other, or to ourselves. I'd say sorry and he'd say sorry, for everything, and we'd

take it all back, all the things said, and he'd reach for my hand
and hold it and look at me, and I'd be filled with remorse for the
things I'd said, and with affection for him. And he'd leave to go
somewhere, training or work or to do a nixer for someone, and I'd
sit and think and my mind would light on something or other
he'd said and I'd start to heat up a bit, and start to bubble, and
boil, and by the time he came back I'd have twisted all the calm
logic of hours before into a new and ferocious weapon to use on
him: Other people? Other *fucking* people? What other people?
And he'd always look shocked, always, no matter how many times
this happened in only slightly varied ways, and I'd rage and rage
that he was a bastard, a bastard, a dirty rotten bastard, and he'd
hang his head in sadness and in shame, and he having, at that
stage, committed no great sins.

Here's how I found out that Pat had been going to the city to see
prostitutes. There was a leak from under the shower in the
en-suite, a circle of damp bulging darkly on the kitchen ceiling.
Pat was just stepping out of the shower; I heard the screen sliding
back on its wobbly rail. I shouted up the stairs to him about it.
Shite, he shouted back. I'll get JJ to have a look at it.

   I picked his phone up from the mantelpiece and said, I'll
fucking ring him myself because I know you never will, and I
heard a clatter, a crash, a shouted curse, a pounding of feet, and
seconds later Pat was naked, red-faced, wide-eyed before me, and
wasn't it just his most awful luck that he'd hidden the madam's
number behind JJ? The universe, Pat, or dead mothers watching
you, long fingers pointing, a cold breeze from nowhere changing
slightly the directions of things.

   A soft female voice, *faux*-seductive, slightly breathless: Pat?
Hello, my love.

   And Pat lunged and the phone flew and came to pieces on the

floor and I fell backwards onto the edge of the recliner and it upended and I landed heavily on my side and Pat picked up the SIM card of the phone and his eyes were wild with fear and he put it into his mouth and swallowed it. And he gagged and his eyes bulged and his chest heaved and the SIM card came flying back out of him and it sat in the centre of my hardwood floor in a little puddle of slime, and I reached out with my foot to cover it, to block it from his grasp.

I stayed on the floor. Pat sat down on the couch in his bare wet arse, his john thomas shrivelled in fear and guilt, receding, attempting to hide itself inside him. And he sighed, and his shoulders sagged, and he spilt his guts.

The woman on the phone looked after a group of girls inside in the city. Not street-girls, like, not them old horrible yokes from the Dock Road: it was a proper operation, clean and hygienic and all. He wasn't sure when it had started. It was just a bit of craic, messing, just a mechanical thing it was, something for the thrill, like paragliding out foreign behind a speedboat, or doing a line, or picking a fight with a knacker. It was just sex, like, we weren't even allowed to kiss them.

We?

A few others from the club. How many times? I never found that out. Once or twice. A handful, no more. Oh, maybe a half a dozen. A dozen at the very outside. I stopped at the dozen, not wanting or needing any more. How many different girls? The same one every time. By chance or arrangement? What difference? True, I suppose. One girl twelve times, two girls six times each, it was plenty, it was more than enough to be going on with. Enough to fashion a scalpel from to silently flay him, the boy who'd strode from the pitch one glistening evening, years before, pointing at his heart, pointing at my heart. The boy who'd grown to adulthood beside me, curled around me, stunting himself, stunting me, a twisted tangle of boughs, hunched and bowed and facing inwards.

I knew he wanted to do penance, to be scourged by me, to cleanse himself; he wanted badly to suffer for what he'd done. He was mortifying his flesh with truth, my husband, throwing himself raw and exposed on the ground at my feet. He wanted to be scalded, to burn his sins in the fire of my rage. So I said nothing to him, not a word, just rose from the floor and left him sitting crying naked on the couch.

My mood is lifted this past few days; this writing down of random things is lightening me, pushing me outwards, creating a tension in me that seems to be serving as a kind of exercise, a tearing and reconstituting, a building of something. I'm not as nauseous, and there's a warmth inside me, and the panic I felt is gone, and so is the idea that I did all this towards an end, to force myself into the abyss. Or the memory of that is fading, at least. It's over three weeks since I told Pat I was pregnant. I wonder where he is, what he's been doing, how much of our story he's told his parents, why he's tried to ring me only once or twice.

Today at the crossroads I inspected myself and deemed my colour to be normal, so his first words won't be that I'm pale as a ghost, so I turned for my father's house though I longed to turn instead for the halting site, and I don't even know why. To see that girl again, to hear her speak. To hear an echo of my baby's father in her voice. There's some notion in my mind that won't come fully to the surface, about being unshackled from convention, about being free and wild and saved. Some stupid thing.

My father was standing, as I knew he would be, at the living-room window, bent-backed, looking out into the drizzle, up at the massing clouds. How much of each day does he give to standing there, looking at weather, watching for me, to stopping himself driving over to me for fear he'd be imposing in some way? And I less than a mile away. And he longing just to see me, to know that I'm okay, because he can't help worrying about me, because he can't help loving me, the same as he did when I was a baby, and a little girl, and a teenager, and a bride, and a woman, and I never having done one earthly thing to deserve his perfect love.

Hello, love, is it yourself is in it? Well, you're as welcome as the flowers of spring, so you are, come in, come in and sit down. And his movements seemed slower than when I saw him last, briefly, nearly a month ago, and he took the bag of messages I'd brought and told me I shouldn't have, to take them away home for myself, he had plenty in the house, oh, Lord, he had.

We sat down at the table in the kitchen to wait for the kettle to boil and my father spoke unbrokenly to fill the air between us. I went as far as Thurles this morning. I picked up a man on the road that was thumbing a lift. He gave the whole journey to giving out about his wife. She was gone from him, I think. Or was he gone from her? Either way, anyway, all the one. Now, says he, and we passing The Ragg, what do you make of that? I have only the one side of the story heard, says I, and couldn't make a judgement. He had a puss on him then for the last few miles, and hardly looked back at me when he jumped out all of a shot below in Liberty Square. And I still rolling, just about. He nearly lifted me out of it, the slam he gave the door. Gor, people do be fierce quare. More so these days. People get wicked vexed unless you agree away with them. There's no countenancing argument any more. Anyway, anyway. Ah, boys.

And he leant forward as though to stand, but sat quickly back again in his chair, as though he had remembered suddenly a plan to conceal from me the rising pain in him and the slowness of him, the stiffness threatening to seize him completely. Only to stop me worrying, everything always for me.

I said, Are you okay, Dad?

And he said, I am, love, I am. Oh, gor, I'm the finest.

I asked him was he stiff and he said, Yerra, no more than usual.

I told him I'd make the tea, and he said, Oh, do, oh, do, good girl. Thanks, lovey. And his voice cracked and broke to a soft sigh, trailing away as I went to the stove.

From the side of my eye as I passed him I saw his hand, thinner than last time, thinning by the week, by the day, I'd say, going to his eyes, and I think that he was crying. I reached the stove and stood there unmoving, my back to him, one hand on the handle of the kettle, and listened and waited and gave him time, humming, pretending I knew nothing of his tears' silent betrayal of him.

A long minute passed. I hummed all the while. Then his voice came, flat, careful, scarcely above a whisper; I listened without turning.

I'll go out, while I think of it, and bring in the bins from the road.

Okay, Dad, I'll pour out your tea for you.

Thanks, love, he said. And still I didn't turn to him. I allowed time for him to lift himself unseen from his seat and hide from me the awful effort of his rising.

A procession of crying men. I'm not even beautiful. I have a good shape, I know, and I'm passably pretty when I make some effort, and I'm young-looking. I have good skin, most of the time. What is it in me that breaks them down? I'm bad, for sure. There's no kindness in me. I can feel it, and think about it, but I can never act it, or be it, the way my father is, the way he's selfless without effort, a man who has kindness in the marrow of his bones, a soul with barely a blemish. I know what it would take to be good, I knew all along, but I never could. I was always this way. I turned from my father's love as a child and only now am turning back to it, now that there is nothing else that I can do. I abandoned Breedie Flynn to the flames. God help me, I did. I don't know why I'm the way I am, or even why I am. I can't see purpose to myself, nor could I ever.

Breedie Flynn should still be on this earth, a scientist or surgeon or actress or comedian or writer of great novels, but I chose others over her, and turned my face away from her the only time she asked me why, and I knew she would have been thinking about me in her last moments, as vain as that sounds, because I knew how she loved me and how I had broken her heart. I could have saved Breedie Flynn. But the cool girls hated her, and I couldn't be one of them if I was Breedie's friend, and I couldn't keep Pat without being one of them, and so I joined in the casting out of her, the daily drawing of her tears. I told them things she had told me underneath her duvet, holding my hand in hers, and when she said, Do you promise, Melody, you'll never tell anyone? I kissed her wet cheek, and stroked her hair, and promised. And those awful secrets were chalked onto blackboards and markered onto whiteboards and graffitied on walls and toilet doors all over our school, and Breedie Flynn's universe shrank about her to a singularity of searing pain. Maybe she'd have done it anyway, at some other time, in some other way, or maybe everything would have been as it was regardless. But I was part of it. I became one of the demons with the goading sticks.

Week Seventeen

I WENT TO the halting site again today, and drove right in this time, before I'd even thought about what I would say to the people I might encounter there. I parked near the entrance and walked across the track and up the steps to the girl's door. I knocked and there was no answer and no sound from within. A pack of wild children surrounded me as I got back in my car. It wouldn't start. Just a click, followed by nothing.

Open her up there till we have a look for you, a small boy, wearing a white button-up shirt hanging loose over tailored trousers, as though he was in the process of dressing for a wedding, instructed me. He had an uneven bowl-cut and a chubby, freckled face. He had the didactic, machine-gun voice of a barroom braggart and the insouciant swagger of a seasoned villain. I pulled the lever near my foot to release the bonnet. He dived under it and emerged seconds later with the bellowed diagnosis: The battery is shorted out, missus. Don't worry wan bit. I'll sort it out for you, no prollum. He looked hardly old enough to be out of nappies.

And sort it out he did. There was too much play there round the battery, missus. The contacts was hitting off a that bit a loose metal there hanging off a the inside a your bonnet. I have it fixed up lovely for you now. I have it wedged in grand and tight now. I done a rale nice job on it. I'll jump her for you now. Wait there till I get my daddy's van and his jump leads.

And as he crossed the rutted ground with a ragtag band of brothers following behind, the door of the girl's wagon opened and she stood there, as startling as she was before, but with her braid undone, her tight jeans replaced with baggy tracksuit bottoms, her face swollen and her eyes red from crying. I went into her pristine home and sat on a plastic-covered couch before a gleaming Formica table. She stood at the far end of the tiny room, looking out the window. My little big man had somehow manoeuvred a huge white van alongside my stricken car and was joining the two engines with a black and red lead, like a four-headed snake, while his companions climbed into and out of both vehicles, shouting commands at one another. I asked her what the matter was.

Not one thing the matter only I gets wicked hay fever.

You have a lot of fresh flowers in here for a hay-fever sufferer.

You're too smart for me, miss.

Please, call me Melody. Why were you crying?

It's only something stupid. My sisters all went off to town earlier on to look at bridesmaids' dresses for my cousin's wedding an I wasn't left go. What a thing to be crying about. I'm not even wan a the bridesmaids. I just so badly wanted to go to town. Just for a look around. To be out, like. Doing normal things.

You can come into town with me now, if you want.

I can't. There'd be murder. I'm been watched ever single second.

Why did your sisters leave you out?

I'm a shame to the family.

And she told me a story, and I listened, and I didn't interrupt her once. Her name is Mary Crothery, and she's nineteen years old.

Mary Crothery speaks in streams, and her speeding tongue sometimes trips itself. She said: I'm a disgrace over the way I left Buzzy. That's the way it's always said. I ran from him. Mommy has my sisters and cousins all told have not a thing to do with me. I'm a bad example. They was all mad into his brothers an all. That's all gone now, and they're like bitches with me. I caused awful trouble. It's hurtful, been ignored. I never knew they'd be able to hurt me so much. I'm the eldest and all. It should be I who decides who gets hurted and who gets petted.

My first night back my little Margaret and Bridget come in to me and lay their heads in my lap and axed me was I all right and gave me beautiful crocheted blankets and bootees and all that they had made for the babbies I never had and my heart near split in two when I saw them and we was all hugging and even my baby brother stood outside the door looking in with sorry in his eyes and it just all felt so nice and safe but the very next day I was froze out and hardly looked at since. I know well what happened. Mommy turned around and said to them I was after making a show of the whole family and landing us in desperate trouble with the Folans and I wasn't to be looked at again till she said so and there was no one to be going in to that lady petting her and seeing is she all right, there's a fear a that wan, she's to be gave no hop and that's all there's to it. I can hear her say it the very same as if the words were said straight into my own ear. She's no sister to ye, that wan, she's no good of a sister.

Remember that tree they chopped down outside the church

in Rathkeale and there was Our Lady inside in the middle of it? We was all been took to see it wan day not so long ago, me and Margaret and Bridget and my cousins Mary-Anne and Mary-Marie and Margaret-Mary and all their children and all the boys and all, and we was to see the tree stump with the apparition of Holy Mary and say a prayer over it for the dead Martins and Nana and Granpappy and all the other faithful departed, and everyone was loaded up into the jeeps and the vans and Mommy's car, and at the very last minute before we left, Mommy come tearing out with a face on her like a bulldog, saying, She's not to be brung, that wan isn't to be brung, and she pointing over at me and I sitting in the back of her car in between Mary-Anne and Margaret-Mary and two childer on top of me and I had to get out and there was a woeful tatter-ah and Pappy was saying, Ah, Jaysus, would you not leave her come? and Mommy was saying, No, no, there's no space, there's no space, I'll get done for there been too many inside in the car, but I knew well it was because she was still horsing over me running away from Buzzy and bringing disgrace on all our heads. My heart was scalded watching them drive off, and Mary-Anne and Bridget and Margaret and Mary-Marie and Margaret-Mary and all waving and blowing me kisses and roaring laughing at me and I standing there, done up to the nines in the empty yard. I cried floods and I a grown woman. And then again today with the trip to see the bridesmaids' dresses. It's the terrible feeling of it, like I'm nothing only a laugh to them now, like my heart don't matter.

What heart matters? I felt like saying to her, but didn't. No heart matters to this mechanical unrolling of happenings, this blind spearing time. We're all tied to the tracks.

She told me I had lovely eyes, and she asked me when was my baby due. I'm four months gone, I told her, and I asked her how she knew. I haven't started to show yet.

She told me she just did. I have a taste of the vision, she said. I got it from my nana. It skips down a generation, always. None of my aunties has it, nor my mommy. I always knows when a girl is expecting, before she knows herself. And I know when there's trouble on the way: I feel it like an aching in my chest, a heaviness of dread.

I know heaviness, and dread. A weight of emptiness, of longing, to be touched, to be lost. I didn't tell Mary Crothery, though, because the time I felt it was the morning of the day I lost my mind with Martin Toppy and I put my hand to his hair as I leant over him where he sat tracing sentences and reading them slowly, and then to his face, and when he looked up I told him with my silence and my eyes that he could kiss me, and he did, suddenly, and he stood and ripped my blouse open, and we had sex on the floor, and again in my bed, and once again before he left, promising to kill any man for me, and that he'd always love me, more words than he'd said in one sentence to me in all the year I'd taught him.

He was so like Pat used to be, though so physically different. A boy, composed of longing. A boy just, a child, beneath the hard muscle and rough skin; his hands were big and strong but still they were the hands of a child.

What'll we read, Martin?

The Cat in the Hat, miss.

Why?

I like that cat lad. He's an awful messer.

Okay, love, I'd say. And that was how we spoke to one other. I would find my hand on its way to his bowed head to brush his dark recalcitrant hair back from his eyes, to caress his cheek, to feel the heat of him, and would only barely check myself in time, until the last time.

*

So there's my father. And Pat. And Martin Toppy. And Breedie Flynn. And the babies I couldn't carry. There's me, sitting here at my solid oak dining-table in a room washed with sunlight. I'm at the centre of this, this grisly diorama in my head, not in a self-centred way, just for simplicity. My hands are twined together, resting on the table. The table has nothing on it. There's a living baby inside me, sleeping, I think. They're asleep most of the time, by all accounts. I wonder if they dream. What could they dream about? Only darkness, surely, and muted sounds.

Dad, Pat, Martin, Breedie, my dead babies, my dead mother inscribe orbits around me and my living baby, elliptical, decaying, intersecting, so that their distances from me vary. They are attracted to me, to the terrible mass of my core, mechanically, dumbly, like hurtling comets, blindly obeying physical laws, arcing inexorably to their ends. I'm a black hole, a swirling void, and these living people are on my event horizon, and these ghosts have been dragged long ago from their orbits and been atomized.

A day came when Breedie Flynn stood beside my desk, and there were scratches on her cheek and bloody strakes, and a clump of her hair had come loose and was falling in soft strands to the floor, and the girls she'd been fighting with, my new friends, crowed and snorted behind her, and the fellas laughed and called her Crater-face and Dykey Flynn and Breedie-freak-o, and she said, Please, Melody, don't leave me alone like this, and I stayed looking down at my geography book, at the blue-green earth on its cover, and one of my tears landed on the Pacific Ocean, and sat unmoving there.

A day came when I told Pat he was disgusting, and meant it, and he knew I meant it, and shock departed our house, and never returned. He was standing behind me, kissing my shoulder, his hands around my waist, one travelling up, one down. I shrugged hard the shoulder he was kissing and felt bone connecting with soft flesh and teeth.

Jesus Christ, Melody, what the fuck?

Oh, get off me, you're disgusting, I said, and I whirled to face him. His mouth was half open, his index finger was running slowly along his upper lip; his mind was sending words but they were delayed, caught in a synaptic jam of surprise and confusion and sudden pain.

Am I? was all he said in the end. Am I really? And it was a proper question.

I whispered my answer, through clenched teeth. Yes, Pat, you are. You're fucking disgusting. And there it was, said and heard, meant and believed, and so never would be shocking again, and we were free then to allow ourselves every vulgarity, every depravity; our language became degenerate. We really indulged ourselves. We let our rage become this mad, living thing. It became our child, our pain incarnate.

Week Eighteen

OH, YES. I'M going mad, obviously. Or I've gone mad. Pat's mother told me that today. I was always a bad bitch but now I'm a mad bitch as well. A mad, bad bitch. And a whore, by the way. Pat spilt his guts, then. He held out a long time. It's six weeks since I told him about the baby. Agnes said: Some dirty rotten fella off of the internet, imagine.

I nearly said, It wasn't, Agnes. I only said that to Pat so he wouldn't get himself killed. It was the Traveller lad I was teaching to read, and I couldn't do a thing about it. I was helpless before it, like a child standing on a shoreline, back to the water, knocked and grabbed by a rushing wave. You know yourself how it is. Go on now, Agnes, go on away out of it, I've enough of you and your progeny. Go on away and don't be fucking tormenting me.

But I let her rave on, thinking: I owe her this at least, the sadness I've brought to her door. She'd let herself in. I think I screamed when I met her in the hall. I'd been sick again, the tail end of the storm, and the toilet wasn't finished flushing. Her eyes went up and down me twice. She licked her lips, tasting the air, testing it. She crinkled her beak of a nose. She addressed my midriff. She started to speak in a near-whisper.

I said nothing for years after ye were married, though I knew well you gave him a dog's life. How is it at all we let him marry you? I had Pat well warned, my lady, that you'd be trouble. He married beneath him. I told him he was marrying beneath him; several times I told him when ye were engaged. I done my damnedest to bring him to his senses. Oh, you had your charms all laid out before him from day one, you were wide open for business with my poor gom, I have no doubt. Sure hasn't the truth of you been well told now? Oh, Christ Jesus, when I think of it! Expecting for some dirty rotten yoke off of the internet! And you not able to keep one safe inside in you for my Pat. Well, do you know what? Thank God. Now! Thank God there's no child involved, only the thing you're carrying now, and with the help of God, and if there's any justice, you won't be left carry it long. Don't you dare look at me like that, lady. Don't you even think of judging me. Lord, isn't it a fright to God to say my Pat married dirt, after all the years and expense of rearing him?

And she looked at me with her spindly eyebrows raised, as though waiting for me to agree, before reinforcing once again that I was . . .

Dirt.

Mary Crothery said: Buzzy paid for rakes of scans and tests and all, to see could they find out what was wrong to say I couldn't get pregnant. We done it night and day from the very minute we was on our honeymoon to the day I ran from him. I loved him, miss. I didn't mind one bit doing it with him the whole time. I got fierce sore once or twice, down there, like, but I didn't say anything the way he wouldn't be getting vexed. He had a real odd way of showing he was vexed, smoking fags one after the other and sitting in the van watching television, real stiff and straight, with a wave off of him that told anyone near him to not bother opening their mouth, they'd be gave no hop. But never once did he raise a hand to me, or call me a name. I seen girls on that site been drug around by the head of hair and bate stupid over the smallest of things, dinners not been cooked right, or some insult only the man could see and no one else. Buzzy was as hard as iron but still and all he was soft with me and he was good to me.

Like, there was an agreement made before we was wed. I wasn't bought or sold or anything like that, but there was money changed hands and some agreement was come to as regards the sharing out of work that wouldn't of been done otherwise. It favoured Daddy and the boys and meant Mommy got a load of things she was wanting for ages. That's all up in a heap now over me. A fella started talking to me at a wedding of a cousin of mine in the north of Ireland one time and this was before I was ever with Buzzy and the fella was putting his arm around me and telling me I was gorgeous and trying to grab my phone off of me so he could ring himself to have my number and Buzzy come along out of nowhere and told your man I was his fiancée and your man gave one look at him and said he was terrible sorry, he was only talking to me, and asked me wasn't that right, and I said it was and Buzzy looked like there was nearly steam coming off of him and your man walked off shaking and that was the first I knew then that I was to be married, and I wasn't yet sixteen, and by the end of that year I was living in a van with Buzzy in a place called Kent, beyond in England. The garden of England, they calls it. There wasn't too many flowers on that site, though.

*

Agnes said: He had a strong line going, you know, with one of the Walsh girls, and at least one farm of land coming to her, and her father and mother good respectable business people inside in town and she indentured in her uncle's practice inside in the city and all. Lord God, when I think of it . . . They'd have made a gorgeous little family. Oh, my heart was solid scalded when I saw him bowling up the path with that stupid grin on his face and you hanging off of him and my lovely Barbara Walsh cast aside like . . . like . . . a piece of . . . *rubbish*! I couldn't lift my face above at Mass for years after for fear I'd meet her mother's eye. I had him told you were a tramp. I had Paddy told. I said the dogs on the street wouldn't sniff you for sport. I told him, so I did, that we'd be a solid show opposite the neighbours having anything to do with the likes of you. I told my Pat. She's beneath you, I said. You got your way, though. You have him squez out now and pure solid destroyed. You took all from him. My Pat, my poor eejit, you have his heart and soul in ribbons, and his life in tatters, and he hardly able to lift his head. Oh, Lord Jesus, when I think of it . . . Oh, Lord God.

And she sobbed and paused again for breath and to dab her eyes and blow her narrow nose and I opened my mouth to tell her all about her poor eejit, her lovely boy, my golden man, my perfect blue-eyed love, and the hours he gave to watching porn on his laptop, getting all sorts of ideas, going into the city and giving it all he had, giving her a good seeing-to, giving her the beans, buried in her up to his bollix, and afterwards, sweaty and red, panting, putting his trousers back on, waiting for a smile, or a kiss at least, some small mitigation, from the dark-haired pummelled girl spread along the low bed, rearranging herself for the next comer.

Mary Crothery said: You can come here any day you like. Whenever you're lonesome. I do be fierce lonesome too. There's

not one bit of shame in it. I'm forever on my own. My mommy
don't bother with me even only to drop in bags of messages and
tell me I'm no use. I'll mind that book for you the way I can say
you're learning me reading if Pappy or Mommy axes. I have it put
away there in the top press. I'll say you're from the council. That
you was sent to make up for the way I was left leave school with
neither word nor number inside in my head. The very minute I
seen you I knew you was kind. That's the why I told you all that
about Buzzy an' all. Don't tell it to nobody, though. When'll you
come back to see me again?

I'm not sure if I'll be able to, Mary.

Course you will. You're very pretty, miss. What's your name
again?

Thanks, Mary, so are you. Melody Shee.

That's a gorgeous name, so it is. And she blushed and pulled
the braid across her face again as I left, and said: We're the same
as wan another, you know, you and me.

Agnes said: And what about your poor widowed father? I don't
know, you'll be the death of him, the poor misfortune.

I'm not sure exactly what I said then, but it was something
along the lines of: Agnes, you know Pat hates you, don't you? And
Paddy hates you. Fidelma tried to kill herself because of you.
You're a cunt, Agnes. You had all their lives well ruined long
before I came along. And the Walshes wouldn't have let their
little Barbara marry one of yours in a million years. The likes of
them wouldn't piss on you if you were on fire, Agnes. You're only
a laugh to them, with your kow-towing and your crawling. And
why would you worry one bit about my father? Surely if I'm dirt
it's dirt I came from. He'd rather see me pregnant by a proper
man than by a fucking weirdo like your boy Pat. Look at the
search history on his laptop and see what you think of it. He

always forgets to clear it. He was still wetting the bed when I started going with him. It was I toilet-trained him. And he still to this day cries in his sleep and wakes in a sweat, saying, Go way from me, Mammy, go way from me, Mammy. What that's about I don't know, and it's no concern of mine any more, thank God. Go on away now and cry into your mixing bowl and finish off the fine job you're doing of torturing poor Paddy to death. And come to my door no more. If I ever see your face again, I'll break it.

Her eyes filled then, and she looked ancient, suddenly, and tired. The skin of her face lost the radiance of anger and turned to crêpe before my eyes, shot with creases and tiny lines of red and blue. She turned away from me and the belt of her coat hung long from one loop and dragged forlornly along the ground behind her. She was halfway across to the path where her shit-brown Micra was blocking the neighbours' gateway when I called her name softly, and she stopped.

I shouldn't have said that, Agnes. Any of it. I only said it to hurt you.

And she made a low noise, like a laugh of weary scorn, and she turned back to face me, standing on my doorstep, my arms folded across my chest, above my tiny swell, and her eyes rested there a moment, and my right hand dropped in an unconscious gesture of protectiveness, and she said, I know what it's like to be left without a mother at a young age.

And she stopped, as though to decide whether or not she should continue, but she did, in a low voice, her eyes never on me but fixed on some space behind my shoulder. I always felt that from you, that lost feeling, that weight of sadness, and my heart went out to you. We could have been pals, you know, if you hadn't been such a flibbertigibbet, forever flouncing about the place and tormenting Pat, and he not knowing from one day to the next what sort of a cut you'd take at him. You could have sat down in my kitchen any time and drank a sup of tea and talked to me, sure I'd have been delighted. But look, how's ever, we can't look for water to flow back upstream. What's done is done and we'll agree to differ, and I'll take a promise off of you that you'll leave well enough alone now and let Pat pick up from where he is and see about living his life, and we'll say no more to one another bar goodbye.

And I said, Goodbye, Agnes, and she nodded, and I watched as she shooed a cat from the bonnet of her car, and drove away, the belt of her coat flapping out from under her door.

So that's more than I've done in a long time. Agnes and I are finished now for good and glory. But there was nothing much there to put an end to in the first place. She only ever tolerated me, and I her. Mary Crothery has told me a story and I feel I should tell her a story in return, but what's there to tell? I married the first boy I ever kissed. I went through four years of college without kissing anyone else, or holding another hand, or talking in whispers late at night in a sweat of desire with any other boy. I started to pick at him around the end of second year, and would let him stay in my tiny bed in the student village but sometimes with my back to him, and I'd shrug his hand away and wouldn't return his kisses, and he'd say, What, Melody? What's wrong? What did I do? And I'd never have an answer he could understand, or that I could understand myself. And he'd leave with the breaking dawn to go to his apprenticeship, washed-out and heavy-eyed, and some mornings I wouldn't even say goodbye. But still he stayed with me, and I was terrified of losing him, and we insisted on marrying each other, and lowering ourselves onto a bed of terrible, scalding, comfortably familiar pain.

It wasn't all bad. I'm not all bad. I'm not evil or irredeemable. I've read all of this back, a month of it or more, and I don't recognize myself, but I know I've been truthful. That these words are still extant, tucked inside a folder on my laptop screen, means something. Is it you, baby? Are you forcing my hand from the dark inside of me, the only warm part of me? Are you whispering to me that you want me to tell you a story?

Week Nineteen

NOW HERE I am, spending my days in a caravan, teaching another young Traveller to read, kin of Martin Toppy, who knew him for most of his life, who lived a few bays away from him until he was taken on the road to work. Kin of the child in my womb, she is. Here I am, listening to her talk, because she has nobody to talk to and nor have I, pretending I'm only here to teach her to read, pretending to her mother to have been sent by the authorities. Here I am, sitting every day and listening to her speak, holding up letter cards and word cards and letting the soft sound of her soothe me, by a window that looks onto the Toppy family's empty bay, waiting for him to come back. Is that what I'm doing? There's something very badly wrong with me.

The doorbell rang again today and I was in my dressing-gown, sitting drinking green tea, and the clock in the kitchen was stopped but the sun hadn't cleared the top edge of the back window and dust motes were dancing in its spotlight, so it must have been mid-morning. Two men were standing there, whose faces seemed familiar. One was smiling, one was not, and the smiling one held a clipboard facing towards me, and a list of signatures scrawled along it. There was a sex offender after being given a house in the area. Out towards the front of the estate. Number eleven. What did he do? He was found guilty of having unlawful carnal knowledge of a minor, the unsmiling man said. He has his time served and he applied for housing and he has it got. In our estate, at the expense of the taxpayers of Ireland, of decent hardworking people. But we're not having it, so we're not.

His face was big, shaved clean and red. His eyebrows were tangled together in the middle, raised like hackles, as though they hated each other. He was holding a biro out towards me, and telling me they needed signatures to give to the county council, who had colluded with the probation service in housing this man here, in a private estate, in a nice area, and children no longer safe to play outside.

What children? I said.

What?

I've never seen children playing outside in this estate. I've heard children, in back gardens, shouting and laughing. I've seen the tops of bouncy castles and swing sets. I've seen and heard evidence of children, but I have no proof of them. I wouldn't let a child outside my front door here, the speed people drive at. That'd be a bigger worry for me. Have you a petition for that?

And the smiling man was unsmiling now and the unsmiling man was darkening fast, and his eyebrows had entered ragged battle.

Do you have children yourself? one of them asked, and I said I had three already and was pregnant again, and one or both of them said, Congratulations, and I took the biro out of the big man's hand and threw it into my grass, long overdue its first cut, and I took the clipboard and threw it onto the grass on the other side of them, and they stood there a moment, looking with their mouths open, before backing down from my step and bending to retrieve their things, and when they'd straightened and had turned to leave, I said, Close the gate behind you.

Mad bitch, the smiling man said.

And I said back: You're only fucking jealous of your man in number eleven. I haven't met a man yet who wasn't a sex offender. There should be petitions against all of ye. But they walked on without looking back, and a curtain twitched across the way, and they were gone around the corner to continue with their spreading of the word.

And now I've written all this down and read it back and I'm not sure it really happened, that it wasn't a dream I had. None of it seems likely. Those men were not familiar, their story rang untrue, their faces and their voices are evanescing now, the way dreams do.

Something else happened, besides those men calling, or besides my dream of those men calling. Mary Crothery came to my door. That's a definite fact, a thing that I can say for sure happened. I had a feeling about you, miss, she said. I woke up this morning thinking about you. I said I'd walk down to you. She was wearing a summery dress and a denim jacket over it and runners on her feet and she looked like a doll, and I wanted suddenly to hug her to me and never let go of her again. But I didn't. Can I come in, miss?

Melody.

Oh, ya, Melody. Can I come in, miss? And I stood aside for her and she came in and stood in my hall and she smelt of cold air, fresh and sweet, and we stood and looked at one another, and she said, You look terrible, miss. Melody, I mean. What's wrong with you?

And I opened my mouth to say something indignant and closed it again and cried. And Mary Crothery told me again how she had just a taste of the vision and how that was enough for her to know that there was something badly wrong inside my heart, and she said again that we were the same as one another, we were after getting put together for some reason, to help one another, and there was no going against the power that lays these things down. And she took my hand in hers and led me through the living-room door to the couch and put me sitting, and she told me she was going to make me a cup of tea and that I was to have a shower and put on nice clothes and we'd go into the city because she had her work all done and Mommy was in good form and she wanted to see a coffee shop down by the river that her sisters and her cousins had gone to that had a big huge picture on one wall of Elvis Presley. The King, they used call him, miss. Did you know that? Lord, he was beautiful.

So I drank sweet tea and showered and changed and we drove to town and Mary Crothery sang Elvis songs until I told her she had a lovely voice and she became self-conscious and stopped. Oh, please, Mary, stay singing, I said, but she wouldn't. I can't now, miss, she said. Because you reminded me of myself. Isn't it funny?

Mary asked me to get her a coffacheeno. A cappuccino? Ya, whatever them frawty wans are called, she said. She'd heard her sisters talking about drinking them and she was mad jealous and them little bitches knew it and they was only doing it to rise her, but she wouldn't please them, let on she was mad jealous, and she couldn't understand how they'd got so wicked in them few years she was gone. I looked back at her from the counter: she was sitting watching me, but straight and stiff, unmoving, as though to conceal herself in stillness. She wasn't even looking at the black-and-white Elvis on the wall, twisting, a guitar slung behind him, his eyes cast down, his face impossibly perfect. Around her, weary mothers dragged buggies and bags through the maze of tables, schoolboys sat in sullen groups, crumpled couples sat facing each other, retired, silent. I ordered our cappuccinos from a stick-thin girl with hazel eyes. She told me to sit down, she'd drop them over. She smiled at me and I almost cried at this small kindness. Your bladder is close to your eyes, my father would say. As I walked slowly back to Mary I saw three crones staring blackly at me from a booth by the far wall. My breath hitched in my throat. A Vesuvius of acid erupted chest-ward from my stomach.

Is your wan going bringing them over? Mary spoke without moving.

Yes, love, I said. And her eyes flicked up at the word that neither of us had expected.

Ah, fair play to her. She's rale busy too. She's a dinger, that wan. I bin watching her away there, flying. It's nice to watch some-one working for a change, not to be the one been watched.

Being.

What? Oh, ya. Sorry. Being.

Don't say sorry. I shouldn't be correcting you. I'm sorry.

You should, miss. I want you to. The way I'll have some improvement in myself to show Mommy. That babby'll be hopping now, you know. Coffacheenos do be full of what-youcallit.

Caffeine?

That's the wan.

The waitress brought our coffee and buns and Mary thanked her without looking at her. Her fingers were twined tightly together. I thought of my mother's fingers as she reposed, artfully arranged by the undertaker, an alien rosary tangled and draped.

Mary was saying: Miss, miss, Melody, are you okay?

And when I refocused my eyes I realized that some time had passed. Mary's hands had untwined themselves and her cup had moved to her lips, and she'd had her first taste of cappuccino, and I'd asked for chocolate sprinkles for her because I knew she'd like them, and she had a tiny island of bubbles on the tip of her nose and a beige moustache of foam below it, and I laughed shrilly at the sight of her. The crones who had been staring looked across. Mary started in her seat. What?

And I heard one of the crones say: Poor Pat. Lord, poor Pat.

I rose from my seat. Flickers like sheet lightning lit the edges of my vision. My heart stuttered, then pounded hard in compensation. I felt a familiar tightening and loosening in my temples; a million phantom pins pricked my hands and feet. I was walking towards the crones but I couldn't feel the floor beneath me. Mary was saying: Miss, miss.

Poor Pat? I suddenly screamed. Poor fucking Pat? And when I reached their booth I gripped the edge of their table and leant in close to their leathery faces and said: Ask poor Pat about his prostitutes. Ask him about the little girls from Latvia he fucked inside in Limerick. And while you're at it, ask Ignatius Farrell and Brian Grogan and Padjoe Walsh about the hookers they've all been riding while their mothers were kneeling down at devotions and saying novenas and doing stations of the Cross in thanks to God that their boys are all married to grand girls.

And I stood back and caught my breath for a second before finishing with: I HOPE THEY ALL HAVE FUCKING AIDS!

And my first regret as we walked from there to the street, Mary Crothery gripping my arm lightly and telling me I was all right, to hush now, come on and we go way home, was that she never got to finish her first cappuccino, frothy and covered in chocolate

sprinkles. Why couldn't I have left it? I wish I could be normal,
or dignified at least, and keep my madness to myself.

I can't seem to focus my mind or still my heart: it's palpitating
and irregular and it's frightening me. I must have upset the baby.
I felt a soft flutter earlier, a tiny agitation, and now he's still, sleeping, I know. Is there shouting in his dreams? It was hours and
hours ago: the moon is halfway across the sky now, and still I
can't calm down. Mary Crothery wanted to stay. She wanted to
know what was all that chat about prostitutes. She wanted to know
was that why my husband was gone from me, was he a desperate
bad man altogether, and I said, no, he was just a man, and she
nodded and seemed to accept this, and I drove her home and I
ached, as I watched her unlock her wagon door, to call to her,
Come back, come back to my house and live with me, and tell me
every day that you're my friend. And I'm frightened now that I was
such a show, and I'm frightened about what will be said, and I'm
frightened about what will reach my father's ears, and how his
heart will speed and slow in worry and fear, and how he'll want to
help but won't know how, so will stand at the window, and watch
the weather, and wait.

Week Twenty

THERE WAS A day on a beach long ago. There was sun and it was low in the sky and there was a warm breeze from the ocean. There was a spray on my face from the breaking waves and the tide was coming in but still there was a mile of beach and my mother was barefoot on it and my father's trouser legs were rolled up to his knees and he was holding a kite above his head with one hand and he was backing into the breeze and my mother was smiling, I think, in the shadow of her hat's wide brim, and she was saying, Go on, let go of it, it'll fly, it'll fly, come on while there's a steady breeze.

And my father half turned to look at me at the water's edge and he shouted, Watch this, Melody, and he let go and the kite lifted skyward as he let the reel out quickly and smoothly, and the kite, pink and purple and shaped like a butterfly, with long streamers of blue and gold, danced left and right in a shifting wind before tumbling suddenly downwards, into the wet sand.

For God's sake, Michael, my mother said. You have to keep the string taut, you have to keep moving.

And my father shouted that he'd be in the water if he kept going backwards, as he reeled in the string and lifted the kite to the sky again, and again the wind took it from his hand and he moved along the waterline ankle-deep in foam and the kite soared and the streamers trailed along the evening sky and again the kite was grabbed by some invisible hand and flung towards the ground, where it rested in a tidal pool, its streamers snaked around it. And my mother said, Oh, Michael. And I stood equidistant between them and I watched my father's reddening face as he rewound the string and untangled the streamers from the butterfly's wings and hoisted its flimsy body to the wind once more and watched as it swooped left and right and he tried to tauten the string and to match the kite's switching trajectories to keep it aloft and it crashed again into the sand and my mother said, Oh, forget it, forget it. And she said, Come on, Melody, and she put her hand out to me and when I took it she looked down at me and her eyes were shining and she laughed softly and said, Your poor father, and we turned for the steps to the car park. And I looked back at Daddy, who was still at the water's edge, facing the setting sun, and I saw him snap the butterfly's spine across his knee and toss its broken body to the waves.

A new day came today and when the doorbell rang I was standing in the hallway, as though I'd been waiting for it. Mary Crothery was wearing the same clothes as yesterday, and her face seemed paler but the same light danced in her eyes, and the same sweet cold air came with her through the door. We sat, and faced each other, and ate KitKats. You're wicked cross, miss. What has you so vexed? I suppose I would be too if my fella went off with prosti-tutes. Did you know some of them wans do have worms in their fannies? They do, anyway. My Buzzy would never of done that. You'd want to mind that child you're carrying, though. You can't be getting upset like that, because it'll travel into him. Did you know it's a boy you're having? I was never wrong once yet. Here, I'll prove it to you. Take off your wedding ring.

And it had never once occurred to me to take off my wedding band, and it was tight on me, or maybe my fingers had swelled. But it came off and Mary Crothery reached up towards my face and plucked a hair from my head and tied a knot around the ring with it and she came around and stood beside my chair and held my wedding band like a pendulum above my stomach and said, Watch this. And though her hand seemed to stay perfectly still the ring began to move in an anti-clockwise circle, and Mary Crothery's eyes were closed, and she asked if it was moving, and I said it was, and she said, With the clock or against it? And I said, Against it, and she said, There's your proof that it's a boy you're carrying. And what more proof could I need?

Go on anyway, so. Tell me, she said.

I did a terrible thing once. I took a person's life from them. I told someone I loved them and I listened to all their secrets and I cried with them and then I told their secrets to the world and so they left this world, because they couldn't stay here with the sadness and the shame. I was young when I did this, sixteen, but I knew I was doing evil and I didn't care. I was in love with this boy who was surrounded by a ring of girls who wouldn't let me through unless I paid them something, and their toll was high. I sacrificed my friend to them, she was my burnt-offering, laid charred on their altar, my beautiful Breedie, with her perfect cheekbones and her full red lips and her terrible scars. I loved this boy so much I forgot how I'd loved my friend, how I'd needed her to be my friend, how she'd come each day of my mother's silent final

week to the hospice just to sit alone in a waiting room in case I
wanted a hand to hold, how we'd hugged each other close beneath
her blankets in her bed when all the world was cold around us,
how we'd held each other tight and promised never to let go, how
she was my first love. I wanted to be her, to have her bones and
her height and her hair and her savage wit. I wanted her sadness
because it seemed to me so heroic and romantic, to be so sad, to
have such traumas in a roiling spring, bubbling behind her eyes.
I even wanted her acne, her livid pitted skin, her stigmata.

These might not be the words I used but this was what I told
Mary Crothery and she listened without looking at me, but at a
spot someplace down to my right, and I wondered as I spoke was
she really listening, because most people can't, and I wondered
was she maybe embarrassed by my story, were there things in it
she just couldn't understand, this pretty outcast, this nineteen-
year-old girl, this old woman, barren, useless, spent, this angel?

Oh, Lord, she said. Lord God, that's sad.

And, of course, Pat knew not a thing about Breedie and me and
what had happened. Because all a boy needs in a small town is to
be good at sport. There is no other knowledge. When Breedie
Flynn died there were more jokes and more graffiti, and Sarah
Bridges, our art teacher, broke into screams one morning in
assembly that we were animals, disgusting fucking animals, and
we all deserved to rot in Hell. And a year went by and there was
an inquest and there was some intimation that the drugs Breedie
had been taking for her skin might have some links to psychosis
and a spate of suicides in the UK, and whatever bit of guilt there
had been dissipated, and there was no more graffiti, and Breedie's
name was not spoken again, and she may as well never have
existed.

These are all just bits and fragments, shards; no one can tell

the story of a life or a friendship or a death or a marriage day for
day for day. Imagine the story of my parents, how it would sound
if it was compressed to paragraphs, or of my teenage years before
and after Breedie, or of me and Pat and our life together, from a
punch thrown at a hurling match one sunny evening in 1998 to
an announcement in our TV room in 2015; how much meaning
would be shed in the telling, in parsing years of numberless
separate moments to single lines; imagine the mass these lines
would have to hold, like dwarf stars, collapsed in on their own
completeness, becoming heavier and heavier until they super-
nova and cease to exist. That's what will happen, what's happening: my story makes no sense like this, not even to me, but Mary
Crothery doesn't seem to notice, she seems to know exactly what
I mean. A taste of the vision, she says she has. I want to scream
with joy, the relief I feel, to have her here across from me, watching me with smiling eyes of grey-flecked blue, and then I think of
the moment that will soon arrive when I have to lie to her again,
about the child inside me and the child who put him there, and
all my selfish pleasure falls away.

I miss Pat more than I thought I would. I've been trying to count
the days I didn't see him or speak to him or touch off him or have
some contact with him in seventeen years and the number is low,
a handful of weeks, or less. So that's why. I miss him in the
mechanical way the eye will miss a tree that's been cut down, just
because it's always been there, and it's gone, but the expectation
of its presence lingers. But then. The many nights he stroked my
head until I slept, then slept himself with one arm resting across
me, as though to protect me from something, to ward something
off. Many nights he lay on his side, facing me, saying things to
make me laugh, saying things he thought would make me lie still
and listen and stop thinking. Many nights he leapt about the

room, squeezed into one of my short dresses, makeup daubed across his face, screeching in a staccato voice, and I'd clap and laugh until tears ran down my face and my stomach hurt. One time he stopped his car by a kerb in the city and cried silently, and he gripped the steering wheel until his knuckles were white, and when I asked him what was wrong he said he didn't know.

Some people stay married for lifetimes, decade after decade, great skelps of centuries together until they're almost in the same skin, growing into each other, shrinking to each other's sizes and shapes, speaking with one voice, clinging fast together, dying days or hours apart. Love doesn't come into it. Not the love of cartoon hearts and cards and cakes and movies and ads for things that no one needs; that grisly synthetic thing, that smiling dog. Love is just a word used to explain away the impossibility of this co-existence, the glorious achievement of being together in the same place, of being happy, and peaceful, and calm, and meeting up again at Heaven's gate, and walking hand in hand to the eternal light. Fairy stories. Couples in care homes curled together in fear, of being alone, of being left in darkness and silence, listening for the step of a stranger, too afraid even to use the commode. This happens, people are left like this. It's better this way, to have smashed it all to bits while we're still two separate people.

But then. What does a thing look like that's never looked at? Is it just the particles of itself, piled together, mostly nothingness? That must be how it is. A thing has form only when light is reflected from it into someone's eye, and its image only exists as it's told to exist in a dispatch from the mind, and even then it's a compromise, an agreement between two eyes and two hemi-spheres of a brain, an impression. A thing can exist and never be observed, and never be bathed in light, and be forever formless, resting in the dark. I had to stay with Pat, I had to make him stay with me; I had to make him marry me; I had to, because Breedie

Flynn died so that it might be so. And this is a fact, a thing that exists, and is only now being touched by light and given form. And another fact is that I've failed her, again, my beautiful, beautiful friend.

And then. There's what I said, or screamed, at the crones in the café in town the other day. They'll have bussed it back in glory with the news. They won't believe it of their own boys, of course, but they'll have it that Pat Shee was caught with his pants down, and that's why the wife is gone from him, and she was inside in Limerick drinking tea with a tinker, and she was screeching and roaring about the place, and she was the worse for wear, God help us, and she had to be dragged away from us by the tinker girl that was with her, and she tried to make out everyone else was as bad as her husband, but anyway, that's it, that's why he's above in his mother's the last good while, he was caught inside in Limerick *in flagrante*. He was drove to paying for it, the poor misfortune. The flesh is weak.

My head aches. I'm hungry all the time. My nails are lined with brittleness and a clump of my hair came out with the brush this morning. I think these things are normal. I Googled them and glanced one-eyed at the lists of results. I don't want to know too much. I feel him stirring all the time now, vaulting about his little world, happy and oblivious. I hold the weight of his existence in my left hand, and then my right hand, and I sometimes feel the flesh there swelling out, and I know then that I'm cupping his little body in my palm.

Week Twenty-one

AND NOW THERE'S this. A long shadow came to my door today. I wasn't going to open it, but I thought of Daddy. Maybe it was something about Daddy. A neighbour, worried they hadn't seen him. A garda, with terrible news. But when I opened it Ignatius Farrell stood sideways there. He rested his right hand flat on the jamb. It seemed monstrous, huge and hairy. His face, while familiar, seemed strangely cartoon-like in profile: his nose speared forward while his chin receded sharply to meld with his long and graceless neck. His head swung towards me suddenly and I gasped in shock. I'd last seen him properly at a hurling club dinner-dance maybe five years ago, and since then only in passing, in cars, in funeral queues. There was a new grotesqueness to his features, a reinforced ugliness. His lips were protuberant and wet, his teeth gapped and yellow. His close-set eyes, canine and febrile, flashed and flared.

What the fuck are you going around saying about me? His

words landed wetly on my face. My gorge rose. I whispered: What?

He exhaled beatifically, as if in disappointment, and repeated his question more softly and slowly than before in mock patience, a grisly parody of kindliness. What. The fuck. Are you saying. About *me*?

His gaze crawled up and down me. His long, insectile eye-lashes flicked, like the proboscis of some foul creature. Ducts and valves spumed and spat inside me; flames streaked across my middle. The baby kicked as though distressed. About *you*? I truly didn't know what he meant. His stare was latched on my chest now and I reflexively folded my arms across it. Spittle tended towards drool on his hanging lower lip. Crescents of white crusts at the corners of his mouth, a sickening parenthesis. And I remembered the café, the day of Mary Crothery's first cappuccino, the three righteous ladies I berated.

Aren't you a fine one going around flinging accusations and you up the stick from getting rode by perverts off the internet? He left his mouth open as if to go on but no more words came. He stepped across the threshold towards me. I went to close the door but he was through; he slammed it back against the wall. Glass cracked and timber splintered. I half stumbled backwards, reaching wildly behind me for the hall table, finding only air. If I turned around I'd be running from him. Something stopped me doing so. Aren't you a fine one? Aren't you now? He was only whispering now; his words seemed automatic, unconscious. And the sun filled the doorway behind him so that he loomed in shadow, his shovel-hands out from his sides, as if to close them around me. He was saying, over and over, You dirty filthy cunt.

And Mary Crothery was suddenly there, and Ignatius Farrell was as suddenly gone, and Mary Crothery was asking me who that horrible ugly yoke was, Oh, sorry, I hope he's no relation of

yours, he had a face of murder on him, was that your husband?
Lord Jesus, what happened your door?

And I told her he was a friend of my husband's, and I'd said his
name in the café that day, the day of the Elvis picture and the
cappuccinos and the screaming madness, and she said, Oh.
That'd vex a man all right, getting named that way opposite
people.

And I told her without thinking that my child wasn't my
husband's at all and she said she'd partly guessed as much, and
she said the taste of a vision she was blessed with was only ever
barely enough to get the skin of a story but nothing of the flesh,
and I could tell her if I wanted, she'd never sit in judgement of
me, nor think badly of me, because she knew I was kind, and I
said, I'm not, Mary, I'm not kind, I never have been.

But she insisted, You are, miss, you're kind, I know you are.
You're a bould bitch the way you done the dirt on your husband
but that don't mean you're not kind.

How can I explain my life? So much of it wasn't mine alone.
Once he was finished strutting and I was finished mooning, Pat
and I entered a shared existence; we wrapped ourselves around
each other in a world peopled just by us, all other things lining
themselves along a circular border around us that we crossed only
when we had to, and engaged with all those other things mechanically and without joy. There was no clean air between us, even. I
breathed in what he breathed out and vice versa. The cool girls
fell away, to internships and graduate positions and years in foreign
countries that became lives. Those friends from school were never
friends at all. I went to Dublin once on the bus to stay over with
two of them who were doing Law and Veterinary in UCD and
they acted surprised to see me even though it'd been arranged,
and we went to their students' union bar and they talked among

themselves and to their classmates, and we went to a gig and I drank too much and took a pill a fella gave me, and I lost my phone and myself and I rang Pat's house from a payphone on the quays and his mother answered and she said, Melody? What are you doing ringing at this hour? What do you mean at all, what? And I didn't know what I meant, or what anything meant.

Most of Pat's friends went away as well, or they stayed and worked in the building trade, or fell to drink and indolence. Wild flowers and prickly weeds and clumps of coarse grass took the run of Breedie Flynn's grave, and her mother would go at it now and then with a shears and a trowel but the clipped and tidied mound would soon fall again to disarray and wildness. I finished my degree and my father brought a friend to my graduation so he wouldn't have to sit alone, and I ignored her all day and Daddy was embarrassed and talked too much to try to cover the awkwardness, and when he went to pay the bill in the restaurant he couldn't remember the number for his bank card and I nudged Pat but he said he hadn't a bean, and he hadn't, because there was no obligation that time to pay apprentices for their work, and the friend paid instead and Daddy turned a dangerous shade of red. And all I could think about was how much of each day that summer Pat would give to me. What time he'd finish work and how long it'd take him to get ready to collect me.

Mary Crothery and I sat in sunshine of unseasonable warmth today, on kitchen chairs dragged out to the decking. A skylark hopped about the lawn, and Mary Crothery said, Lord, will you look at him, miss, he's the cut head off a young fella I know that wears his hair all long on top and slicked back with gel! And she laughed a childish laugh, and clapped in delight, and the skylark hopped in fright and flew away, and she watched him flit skyward with wonder on her face. And I looked at her and felt something

like love for her, a strange intense tenderness, and a feeling that
she was in some kind of danger, and that I was somehow making
things worse for her. They're all cousins on the site, she'd told me.
Martin Toppy is her kin, her clansman. What would she say to
the rest of my secret? More than, You're a bould bitch. Your
husband's a soft man, she said earlier, to have left you standing at
all. If I'd of done to Buzzy what you done to your fella he'd of
buried me. And there was a whisper of pride about this, as though
she'd think less of herself if she'd been married to a man who'd
leave an adulterous wife above the ground. Who pays for this
house now? she asked me. And I told her it was my house, I'd
bought it with the money my mother left me, that she had been
left by her parents, that had sat in a trust for a lifetime because she
couldn't bear to use it. Why couldn't she? I didn't have an answer.
I don't know why. There had been something in her family, some
tenebrous unmentioned thing that acted tectonically along its
fault lines and opened a vast schism of silence between them. So
I just said: She was mean. And I didn't feel bad saying it, because
she was.

All you are to me is a tenant, I'd say to Pat. And he wouldn't
answer. A tenant who pays no fucking rent. And he'd open his
wallet and throw whatever was in there at me. And he'd stuff a
gear-bag with jeans and shirts and socks and boxers, and slam the
door behind him and drive away, and he'd return hours later and
I'd say nothing to him except, You're back, are you? And he
wouldn't answer, and most times I'd just leave it there. I remember a night given to screaming and tears. He'd said something or
done something that had maddened me. God knows what. I only
remember that night specifically because, as I spiralled downwards to sleep, I thought, What's brought me here? Why am I
collapsing exhausted into bed while Pat sits up downstairs, too

afraid to use the toilet in case it sets me off screaming again? Because I couldn't bear flatness, equilibrium, to exist on a plain, in a straight unbroken line without trough or crest to hide me from myself. I engineered these passions, these trials, to convince myself I was living a life. Even misery was better than boredom. I drove the roads, searching, not knowing for what. I stopped the car one day at Kiltartan Cross, miles and miles from here. Two counties away. I imagined an airman imagined by Yeats, contemplating his inevitable fiery spiral from the sky, and I envied him. I sat on a sodden bench in Coole Park and thought of the torments of writers long dead, and wished for some new torment of my own, to add to my cold mother and my lovely friend, long in their graves; some linchpin on which to hang my sense of myself. I wished for fresh miseries, long before there were miscarriages or prostitutes or blue-eyed Traveller boys at the edge of manhood, sitting in my kitchen shrouded in sadness.

Week Twenty-two

SO HERE NOW am I, this new incarnation of me, this version I never expected, this thing. And I know that I have, I have lost my mind. I feel happiness now in the parts of days where Mary Crothery keeps me company, and I feel safe, somehow, even while my sense that she's in some kind of danger increases. I heard or read somewhere once that all women go a little insane during pregnancy, that the sudden switch from a natural state of physical selfishness to an enveloping vessel for another life causes a shift in consciousness akin to madness. I must be mad, to be able to breathe in and out so freely, to be able to admire the blue of the sky and the daubs of white across it, to enjoy the feel of sunshine on my skin. After all the things I've said and done, after all of that, I'm here, allowing myself these hours of simple pleasure.

The internet says my baby now is fully formed, a tiny version of his born self, downy and fatless and budded, though his eyes have no colour yet. They'll be blue. I wonder where these certainties spring from. They're as real as my thickening hair and my sprinting brittle nails that I have to file daily, as real as my shifting flesh, the skin of my stomach stretched out around my tiny mound. Fate, the idea of it, has substance only in retrospect, yet lately all my moments seem ordained, fashioned by a finger not my own.

I keep wondering where Pat is. I found myself watching out the window for him today. I keep thinking I should ring him, then wonder what I could possibly say. That it's come to this, love. It's come to this and now there's no going back, ever, and aren't we better off? I made it come to this, to save myself, and to save him too, in a way. We both did terrible things, to save ourselves, to save each other, to make it so we'd have to leave each other, to leave each other alone. Now I imagine conversations all the time, words well chosen and softly spoken that could have rescued our lives, our life. Or would they just have been a ragged bandage on a suppurating wound? Pat had sex with prostitutes: that's a fact. I had sex with a teenage boy who'd been left in my care: also a fact. What words spoken could have changed these facts, that we were all along capable of doing such things? Worse things are done by people to each other, but not by much. We perpetrated atrocities. A holocaust we had in our three-bed red-brick house, a wiping-out of love.

Mary Crothery told me more of her story. She couldn't stay in England, in her wagon with her husband in Kent. She couldn't ever have babies because of some fattening of the tissue around her cervix that restricted blood flow and caused a hardening, a formation of dry fissures. She'd learnt this off by heart, this reason for her barrenness, so that she might be excused by her people, by Buzzy's people, if they heard the big words spoken, the proper

medical words, the way the doctor had spoken them. It was no
fault of hers, nothing she could ever have known about, nor her
mommy or daddy, before she was promised to the Folans. But still
she couldn't stay, she said, because Buzzy closed himself off from
her once the final verdict was given, and he hardened himself
against her, and he wasn't able to be any other way because
children are precious things, Mary said. Having children is a
precious thing, and a thing all men have a God-given right to,
and the Lord decreed it that this thing was to happen to her, but
that was no fault of Buzzy's, and he shouldn't be made to suffer
because of the punishment that was handed down to her, she
said, and it wasn't ever said straight out to her face, but there were
strong suspicions, she knew in her heart and soul, that she'd been
damaged inside by some other man, and that the Crotherys had
known all along about the deadness inside in her, and had pulled
a fast one. So it was for Buzzy's own sake that she ran from him,
and they'd been married in England and so could be divorced
there, and there'd be no need to be apart from one another for
four years the way it's the rule here in Ireland, and all she'd have
to do would be sign her name to some papers that would come in
the post to release him, the way he'd be able to find someone else
and have baby after baby, and his heart would be filled, and his
days, with the joy of being a father, and a proper man. And she
closed her eyes when she had finished telling me this, and she put
her hand across her mouth as though to silence herself.

Mary Crothery consigned herself to a life of shame and fear
and exclusion, having caused all this trouble, and expense, and
nothing now to show for it, only the seeds of a blood feud, because
the Folans weren't going to be pacified too easily, it seems, by the
signing of some papers and a note left on the table of a wagon
saying, Sorry.

*

Mary prefers to have lessons in my house. It smells nice, she says, and it's never cold. Wagons is great to heat but fierce bad to hold it, she says. Her mother doesn't let her use the mains connection some days, when she's in a tear of a mood, which is often. She does be forever hopping over money, and roaring over the size of bills, Mary says. There's no letterbox on the door of Mommy's wagon and the postman stopped knocking for a finish to hand her letters to her if he seen one from the electricity crowd, because she took to balling them up and throwing them back at him and telling him he could send them back where they come from, and he said one day she shouldn't shoot the messenger and he laughed, but Mommy didn't laugh back, only said to him real serious with wildness flashing in her eyes: Don't fuckin tempt me. So he started to leave all her letters on her top step, standing leaning against the door, but once or twice they blew off across the site and got drowned wet and she was hopping with temper over it and she lifted him out of it again over that and he ran away from her and drove off in his van that time and hasn't been back since. Now the whole site has to collect their letters from the place in the Dock Road and Mommy has a claim in against the post office because she makes out that them people are discriminatory against us for not bringing the post properly the way they're supposed to.

There are days Mary isn't given permission to leave the site. Mommy is capricious, it seems, in her granting of privileges, and Mary has to concoct all sorts of stories to win her fleeting freedoms. That I have other students besides her. That they were being brought to a talk in the welfare office about filling out forms. So I sat today in her spotless home across a small table from her on the plastic-covered couch and watched her bowed head bob slightly with the rhythm of her reading, and out through the window behind her I watched two small boys fighting, and a ring of men was forming around them. The laughter of the fighting boys was dying with the rising of the numbers watching them, and their punches became more circumspect, their ducks and dives more artful, and their faces set in seriousness, and their aim became more true. One of them was very overweight and they both wore white vests and bright Bermuda shorts, and the bigger one turned in a tight circle as his more sprightly opponent danced in a ring around him, but the bigger one for all his slowness seemed less troubled and better able to guard himself, and after a minute or so he landed a fist on the slighter boy's nose and a splatter of blood reddened both their vests and a guttural noise rose from the ring of watching men as the injured child staggered backwards and almost fell, and gathered himself, and put his guard back up, and started again to dance about. Mary didn't rise from her study of our book, even when the shouting rose to screams; my view was almost fully blocked by cheering boys and men when suddenly the ring broke inwards and the smaller boy was hoisted shoulder high, and his opponent was sitting dazed, his torn vest streaked with earth and blood, two narrow lines of tears cutting through the dirt on his cheeks, and no one was helping him up, but men were stepping over him to lay congratulatory hands on the bloodied victor.

And Mommy descended from her door and the shouts faded as the champion was set down before her, and she bent and put her tanned and bracelet-laden arms around him, and she kissed him on his cheeks and said something to him that made him smile and redden and cast his eyes embarrassedly downwards, and some of the men behind him clapped his back. And the loser was on his feet now and someone ruffled his hair, and Mommy climbed the steps to her door again, and I knew in that instant exactly what Mary Crothery's place was in this narrow world: I realized the extent of her shame. Sent home husbandless from

England, a broken promise, a living debt that could be repaid only in blood. And I thought: These people don't deserve her. I thought: She should be mine. I thought of her, in that shocked moment, as a chattel, a thing that I could own, and when her blue eyes left her book and met with mine I was burning with shame. At last, I felt ashamed.

Mommy's mood seemed almost wildly happy, she having watched her son cut his teeth and draw his first blood. She asked me as I left today had I seen the fight, and I said that I had, and she said, I suppose you think we're animals. But that's the way of things for us, and we're more noble than you know. I'm proud of what that boy done today. Don't be going off now back to your office telling tales about anything you seen here. It's no one's business. And your only concern around here is giving that wan what she was never gave in school. And she pointed from me to Mary and up at the sky, in invocation of God, or watching ancestors; I don't know. Before I could answer she turned and walked away from me, throwing an unreadable look towards Mary, standing in her trellis frame. She stopped and turned back, as though something had just occurred to her, and said: I hope you'll have that wan well taught for me. I goes to awful trouble filling forms, and that's the only use that I can see for her. Mary stayed silent, looking at her mother, her face blank and passive. And Mommy said to her: You can have tomorrow free once the wagons are cleaned. And she turned away again and I admired the sway of her, the queenly straightness of her back, the sceptred sureness of her step.

Mary looked wide-eyed down at me. Can we go to the seaside, miss? To the big one, like. What's this it's called? The Antarctic Ocean?

I knew what she meant, but I said, That's thousands of miles away, Mary, down at the bottom of the world.

It's not, miss, it's only out there if you goes left at Ennis, about forty miles, Daddy says.

That's called the *Atlantic* Ocean, I told her, and she said, Oh, ya, aren't you great the way you knows the names of all these things? Pity you weren't as good at knowing how to keep your knickers on the time you went off with the dirty man. And I widened my eyes and breathed in sharply in mock indignation, and she laughed and said, Ah, miss, I'm only codding you.

Week Twenty-three

TODAY DAWNED FRESH and cloudless and I prayed the rain would stay away all day. I packed a wicker hamper with sandwiches of tiger bread and oak-smoked ham, and bottles of Coke and water, and bars of milk and dark chocolate. I put a blanket and towels in the boot, just in case. I drove to the halting site at midday, and Mary was waiting at the foot of her steps, with a small pink knapsack on her back, and her good jeans on, and her hair braided tightly, ribboned almost primly in pink. I nearly cried at the sight of her, I'm not sure exactly why. The way she was waiting, like a child, happy and excited. She'd only ever been at the seaside once, and she barely remembers it, but she remembers the crooked land they drove over to get to it, the edge of the world, and she remembers the spray on her face from the crashing waves, and the other people moving away from where they spread their towels so that they were an island in the sand, and Daddy had sat bare-chested and silent and her baby brother toddled off and fell against a rock and cut himself, and he roared and roared, and Mommy lost her reason and they had to go home. She'd never again since laid eyes on the ocean. They weren't proper walking people any more. People gets fierce bogged down in sites, Mary Crothery says, and the ease of having water and the power from the mains.

She'd crossed the Irish Sea with Buzzy, but they'd rolled onto the ferry in darkness each time, and she'd been sick the last time and had stayed below deck for the whole crossing. Buzzy had gotten excited, thinking maybe she was sick with a child, and she'd told him she was sure she wasn't: even if she was expecting already there'd be no sickness so early. He'd gotten quiet then and seemed cross, and after a little while he'd come back to himself a bit and had put his arm around her and asked could he get her anything, a glass of milk or a bottle of water, and she'd said no, even though her mouth was dry as dust, but she didn't want to seem to be a nuisance, to be dogging him for things and forcing him to wait on her. Then he'd asked did she want to go up on deck and she'd said no, she was too afraid of the way the ship was rolling, they might fall into the water, and he had laughed and said that was nothing at all, there was barely a wave, he'd crossed a few times when the ship nearly turned upside down, and he tightened his arm around her, and she knew this wasn't a natural or an easy thing for him, and it had made her love him even more.

Mary Crothery sat silently beside me as we headed west on the motorway, and the space between us was warm and calm, and didn't need to be filled with words. I glanced at her every now and then and each time saw a hint of a smile on her lips, and I smiled too, at the way her hands lay on her lap, the way she sat leaning slightly forward, straining against the seatbelt, as though willing the car to greater speed, the moments and the miles to pass more quickly.

We parked on the street in Lahinch and walked, our picnic basket and blanket between us, down to the water. Mary Crothery cried when she saw the ocean. She walked slowly towards it with her hands across her face and stopped a few steps from the water-line, her tears mingling with the spray and the salty breeze, and she screeched in delighted fear as a small wave broke and a cuff of foaming water rushed at her bare feet. Oh, miss, she said, oh, miss, I didn't remember it right. I never knew it would be this beautiful.

We paddled for a while in the frigid water, and we ate our picnic with our blanket wrapped around our shoulders against the cool wind, and we sat on the sand before the tide-washed rocks, and we watched the waves and the westering sun, until the blood-red sky fell down across the water and stretched itself along it.

Mary Crothery slept for most of the journey home, turned sideways in her seat with her knees drawn up, and I kissed my fingertips and touched her forehead and she smiled in her sleep like a child.

I stood and watched a black-haired infant, standing by a river throwing stones. High up into the air and his head would rise and fall in following and his laugh when the stones splashed into the glass-smooth water rebounded off the far bank and rang in my ears, like something too beautiful to be of this world. Be careful, little man, I was saying, and I was walking towards him with my hands out, but my legs felt heavy and stiff and he looked back at me and smiled and the sun lit his face and glinted off his eyes and he flung his two arms upwards, and as his pebbles flew away across the waiting water, he wobbled on his little legs and fell, and disap-peared below the bank, and still my legs wouldn't carry me towards him and I woke with the sound of splashing in my ears and a scream on my lips that made no sound because the breath was gone from my body.

I keep these terrors for my sleep. I want the air about me to be still and calm. I check myself daily now, all the parts of me that will change. I watch for the white marks of calcium deficiency on my fingernails and I search along my skin for red spots betraying stress on my liver and I count the beats of my heart for fifteen seconds and multiply the number by four, and I check that the rhythm of the beats is even, a strong and steady sinus. I measure my wrists and ankles around with my thumb and index finger to mark in my mind any changes there. I do these things and then I sit still until I feel him stir and then I do them all again. My bump is tiny and neat and I cup my hands around it and stare at my naked self, and I think of Eve and all the sins done in the world since hers, and of my own sin, and I feel no shame, only a wonder, that I could be standing here, admiring this small warm mound, my perfect swelling.

All the marks we ever made will fade away, and all the memories of all the things we ever did will die, and it will be as though we never existed. There's no more to be done, now that we've committed our terminal atrocities. There's nothing to be felt now but a strangely blunt dissonance, a place without edges or dark corners, a soft, low buzzing in the background, like fabric gently tearing, a world of vague, uncertain shapes and sounds, stretching away behind my naked mirror image, the woman in the glass before me with her thumbs and forefingers touching on either side of her stomach, the space between her hands forming the shape of a heart against her flesh.

I can't bear the thought of being scanned, the cold gel and the friendly smile and the ultrasound machine traversing me, circling, searching for a heartbeat. I remember the eyes of the technician the last time, the downturned lips; she was young and inexperienced and I think she almost cried. She told me not to worry too much and put her hand on mine and with the other hand she rang a bell for help, and a tall and handsome obstetrician came and relieved her of her discomfort. But I'd known, each time, from the blood, the amount of it, the dark clots, the stabbing pangs and the terrible stillness. And I'd shouted up at Pat to get away from me, that he was probably happy, that he was off the hook, and he shook his head and closed his eyes and put his two hands to his face.

I know it would be okay if I went now and presented myself, and asked to be admitted to the system, added to the roll of expectants, pencilled in for scans and checks and reassuring words, for antenatal courses where I could sit cross-legged on a cushion on the floor and chat and laugh and listen to a kind and battle-weary midwife tell us how to use our breasts. I can feel him and I know he's strong, but I felt a dull pain low down beneath my bump last night and my knees buckled in fear and I had to lean against the hall table and breathe evenly and deeply till it passed. And I know I have to do this, to leave this town and drive the twisting road to Portiuncula, because everyone here goes to the Regional in Limerick to have their babies, and at least one face in ten would be familiar, and there'd be no way to keep a secret there.

Week Twenty-four

I WENT TODAY to my father's house and I told him. The sky was
split between black rainclouds and piercing, watery sunlight as
I drove, and a rainbow arched above the earth, and I knew my
father would be watching it as he watched out his window for me.
I'd caught an intimation of reproach on the phone, in the moment
after I said, Hello, Dad? A second or maybe two of heavy silence,
and he left it there in the silence, his tiny hint of censure, of course
he did, and there was only relief in his voice when he said, Oh,
love, what way are you at all?

And I said, I'm fine, Dad, I'll be out to you tomorrow. Do you
need any messages?

And he said, No, love, I'm well stocked. Begodden I am. I've
plenty. What time will you be here about?

He was standing at the window as I turned into the yard, and
the grass on the front lawn was longer than he'd ever let it grow in
my memory, and the evergreens against the fence were growing

out towards wildness, and the beds had all been taken by the grass. Daffodils bloomed in unruly ranks along the borders, vying with the weeds for space. My mind can measure these things, can note these markers of decline, but my heart can only close itself in fear. How much I need my father to be here, waiting, thinking about me, my lovely quartermaster, in charge of a store of unconditional love. Someday maybe I'll do something to deserve it.

He planted an apple tree at the end of my garden once, when I was pregnant the first time. He patted the earth around it with the flat of his spade, and straightened, and wiped the sweat from his eyes and said, without looking at me: That'll still be here in fifty years, please God. And maybe your child will stand where we are now, or your child's child. And I'll be long turned to dust.

And I had to say, Stop, Dad, please don't talk like that.

And he laughed and said, No one lives for ever. And he sat on the garden bench beside me and held my hand a few weeks later and said nothing at all, about life or death or anything else, because he was afraid to speak, I knew, because he couldn't trust his voice, or the waiting tears to stay unfallen.

We sat today and I drank inky coffee from the French press, and he drank milky tea, and he asked over and over was the coffee all right; he wasn't too sure, you see, was he doing it exactly right, but there was a video of how to do it exactly right on the internet, and he'd followed that, because it was a long while since he'd used the yoke. He only ever drank tea, and anyone that might call would only ever have a sup of tea, but he knew the benefits of coffee, for sure, how it would help you to concentrate if you were tired, for driving especially, Lord, it's great now for anyone driving a long journey, how they can stop off any old where and get a cup of coffee, in a paper cup with a special lid, to bring with them in their car and sip away while they're driving, the way they'd stay alert, and he'd started making it about ten minutes before I was due to arrive because the nice darky lad on the internet said it was necessary to let the coffee – what's this he called it? – oh, ya, *infuse*, and sure he supposed it's the same as letting tea draw.

I'm pregnant, Dad.

And he looked at me and said, Oh, love. Oh.

And I said, It's not Pat's. I had an affair.

And he waited for a long moment to be sure of his voice, and he said, Is it true that Pat's gone from you? Minnie Wiley asked me that before devotions last Sunday evening.

And I said, Yes, Dad. I should have told you earlier.

And he said, You couldn't have news before Minnie Wiley. She'd tell you what you ate for your breakfast. And he looked down into his tea and he sighed, and said, What sort of a man is he at all? To say he couldn't manage things. And I didn't know what to say so I said nothing.

My father described to me his days, as if to put in context how my news might fit with them, or maybe just to be saying something, to dilute the thickness in the air between us. He rises early and unstiffens himself as best he can and he manages the stairs the finest if he takes his time and he watches the birds and the brightening sky from the back window, and he tightens up the place a bit, and he has his tea and porridge and a cut of toast and marmalade, and he performs his ablutions, and he puts on his corduroy trousers and his polished shoes and his shirt and pullover and jacket, and he goes out the door to Mass. He has a bit to eat some days at lunchtime in the café below; there's a grand girl working there from Latvia or Lithuania or one of them places, and she's solid lovely, as nice of a girl as you'd meet, the very same as an Irish girl she is, the way she'd welcome you and ask to know were you all right while you're having your bit to eat and asking do you want a fresh sup of tea. More days he has his lunch at home, a bit of ham or chicken and a hard-boiled egg and a few slices of bread and butter. And he reads the newspapers in the afternoon, *The Times* and the *Indo,* and the *Herald* the odd evening. And he has his dinner fine and early the way he was advised one time, a couple of chops maybe, and a potato, and he looks at the television in the evenings, the news and the weather and whatever match might be on, or a film maybe. And the odd evening he goes down as far as Ciss's for a pint, and those evenings he'll smoke one cigarette before bed, and there was never a man yet killed by one cigarette in a blue moon.

And I listened while he described his days to me, filling the space between us with a picture of a life lived alone but still selflessly, because his only concern, I know, though he'd never say it, is me, and whether I'm okay, and whether I'll ever have a child the way I wanted to, and whether there's something wrong that can't be righted to say I lost two little babies before they had a chance to take a breath, and whether Pat is good to me, and whether I'm any way contented. And what small bit of peace he might have drawn around him in his silent days, in his kneeling at his stations or his watching of a match or his drinking of a pint, is gone from him now, because of me, and my new trouble. And the shake I see now in his hand was put there by me, and the tear that glints in the corner of his eye, and the words that come from his mouth. Don't worry, love. Don't worry. Things always work out in the end.

Oh, Daddy, if only that were true.

I slept well last night and woke looking forward to Mary Crothery's visit. I want to practise writing with her, to see her making letters on a page. Two o'clock came and went without a sign of her. I sat and wondered, worrying the edges of a book. I wish she had a phone so I could text. She had, I think, but it was confiscated as part of the stripping away of her privileges, the punitive diminution of her inflicted by Mommy, who'd never get over the disgrace of it. What that wan done to the family. I drove at the end of the unused hour to the Ashdown Road, and met the mumbling sentry and the ragged swaggering boys, sparring in the spaces between puddles, and one of them shouted, Them is all gone away, ma'am, as I put a foot on Mary's bottom step.

Gone away where?

Dunno, England?

And a burning started in my belly and I felt the baby stir. I read about that happening: agitation from adrenalin injected by sudden stress. I tried Mary's door anyway, and it was locked, and the curtains were drawn across the windows, and my breath caught a little in my throat, and I felt a little light-headed, and I gripped the handrail by the steps for balance. Are they coming back? I asked the boy who'd lost the fight the other week, and he said, Prolly. Spose. Weddin. Tarmacaddanin. And he turned his faintly bruised and sullen face away from me, and he raised his guard again.

I sat back in my car and started for Daddy's, and changed my mind and turned for home. I vacuumed up and down the hall, and changed the sheets on all the beds. I folded clothes Pat's father hadn't taken, and pressed a shirt against my face, and breathed in ghostly sweat and skin. I wondered where he was again, and how he filled the gaps I used to fill. I went in the end to Daddy's, and he wasn't there, and I sat on the concrete bench at the end of the garden and cried, and suddenly he was sitting beside me, and he had a hand on my shoulder, and he was saying softly, embarrassedly: Ah, now, ah, now, you're okay, pet.

Were you in with the doctor since I saw you last?

No, what'll a doctor tell me that I don't know?

Daddy looked at the sky, where he always looks. Oh. Ah, boys.

Would you not go in for a check-up? And I said I would, as soon as they called me with a date and time; I'd asked for an appointment. Oh. Righty-oh. Well, that's good, anyway. And he told me how worried my mother had been, all through her pregnancy, how she'd taken to her bed for days and weeks at a time, and had been as weak as a sop and had had pains head to toe; how he'd stayed at home from work to mind her and got in terrible trouble with his boss because he'd taken holidays that hadn't been approved and they'd docked his pay. How he'd feared so much for both of us because she wouldn't eat for a time and hardly drank a sup of water, even, and lay still with the curtains drawn and barely spoke, until for a finish he'd fetched the doctor and he'd come to the house and told her sternly that she had to buck herself up, that there was nothing medically wrong with her, that she had to eat properly and drink water, and the doctor gave her tablets to take and a page of writing that she would study intently and never let her husband see but he thought it was a list of things she had to do, and things she had to eat, and she lifted herself out of it for a finish and everything was grand afterwards. That's the way of things, sometimes, my father said. Things happen inside in a person that they think they have no control over, and it turns out they do, but they need to be told by someone else.

I read a book about a man who lives alone in a small house in a small town that was almost destroyed by war. And his neighbours and his childhood friends set upon each other, and the love of his life was killed. And after the war was over, the town and the people left living there had to continue living, watching all about them through uneasy eyes, remembering and thinking always but never speaking of the things that happened. I feel a kinship with that imagined man, living where blood once ran, surrounded by the echoes of screams.

Week Twenty-five

PAT CAME TO the door yesterday, just as the light was starting to fade. Hello, I said, in an unintentionally interrogatory tone, like a telephone greeting, like I didn't know him. He stood, hunched and stooped and streelish, and his arms hung long by his sides. He looked older, and had lost weight, and his hair seemed thinner on top.

Long seconds passed, until he said: Sorry, Melody. Sorry. I shouldn't of said I'd kill you.

And I replied: Shouldn't *have*. Confusion flashed in his eyes, then recognition, of that old familiar correcting, my bitch-reflex, working unbidden. He reddened still more. His face shone. And I wished I had razors for teeth to cleanly slice from me my wicked tongue. I knew he didn't know what do with his hands; so, unthinking, I took one in mine. He opened his mouth, in shock at my sudden gesture of tenderness or to speak, I don't know, but no words came. So I just said, It's okay.

Just that, and he smiled a shallow smile in reply, a bare upturn of the corners of his lips. His eyes lowered to my bump; a shadow caressed his face. He gently reclaimed his damp hand and stepped back, turning for the narrow, weed-lined path, mad zigzags opened along its length by rain and frost. He was wearing the Levi's I bought him a few Christmases ago. They bagged unbelted around his narrow arse. His sloped shoulders were hunched; his half-ironed shirt billowed mournfully from his bones in the rising breeze. He looked back from the garden gate and waved, and lingered for a second, and turned away from me.

I stayed standing at the door looking out and across at the obsessive-compulsive gardens of my neighbours: lozenges of unstained tarmac flanked by ranks of straight-edged plants. How many of them know? Someone was looking back from a house directly across and down a bit, towards the bend. Mrs Brannigan. Or Flanagan. Or some-fucking-thingagan. And I watched Pat walk away. And I called him back.

He spun on his heel the second I called, and was back through the gate and in the door before I could register properly what I'd done. And he stood in the hall and said, What'll we do? And the question was at once strange and familiar. And it felt for a moment like it felt when we were seventeen and we'd only started having sex and we found ourselves in a private place where we couldn't be heard and there were no parents about and no possibility of them for a known and definite length of time. When we were seventeen he'd say, Come here, and I'd say, Just a shift, that's all, and he'd say, Ya, I know, and within five minutes we'd be in my room or his room, naked save for our underwear, and he'd fumble and curse at the clasp of my bra, and I'd take it off for him and he'd say, Thanks, and I'd say, Jesus, and we'd writhe in sweat to a burning point and I'd say, Fuck it, go on, go on, but make sure and pull out in time, and we'd gasp together as he entered, and

I'd gouge furrows in his arse with my fingernails, and he nearly always would pull out in time, with tenths of seconds to spare, because he'd have waited for me, saying the alphabet backwards in his head or thinking about the naked bodies of his grand-mother's friends, and the sheets of the bed would be destroyed and folded carefully, sticky patch inwards, and smuggled to the bottom of a laundry basket, and we'd dress ourselves and lie on our backs holding hands and talking about God knows what, and sometimes if our time allowed we'd do it all again.

My father walked into my room once on an early midsummer afternoon when we were both asleep, naked, covered only by a sheet. Pat had cycled round that morning when the house was empty but for me and my mother's ghost, and she never bothered us. We'd thought we had hours yet. But Daddy had left in a hurry that morning and he hadn't packed a lunch and so he'd come back just after one and he'd noticed clothes strewn on the stairs and he'd picked them up and he was holding them in shaking hands and looking down at us when I woke up and said, Daddy, what the *fuck*? and I pulled the sheet tight around my nakedness and Pat woke then and laughed in panic and Daddy said, Oh, sorry, cripes, I thought there was no one here, I was only tighten-ing up the place, your clothes were left on the stairs, and he looked down at his hands and it was Pat's Chelsea jersey he was holding, and my bra, and my skirt, and he dropped them onto the foot of my bed and he said, Anyway, anyway, ah, boys, and he was red from his neck to the top of his lovely head as he retreated, and Pat and I looked at each other and laughed into our pillows and listened for his leaving so we could do it again.

And I think, because I know him, and I know just how he thinks, that Pat was thinking too about those times, when all the world seemed fashioned to our love. When all the secrets of our bodies were freshly discovered, and known only to us, and even the rain against the window seemed to beat time to our rhythms, and people smiled on the street when they saw us holding hands, because we seemed to fit the world and each other and the space we occupied so perfectly. But we knew it was the world that fitted us, that everything else that existed expanded outwards from us, and was futile and empty of meaning.

Pat shrugged, and he laughed, a tiny exhale of a laugh, and he looked at the ceiling and clicked his tongue. That damp is spreading. Fuck it. Out across to here now it's gone. It'll fuckin fall through. And I said nothing in reply and we stood in silence, and it felt like a warm coat around me that had been lost for a time, that had been tailored to my shape and worn daily for years, so easy was it just to stand wordless in the hallway with him. And he looked so like his teenaged self I laughed, and he smiled and looked at me, expectantly, as though my next words would contain a panacea, an undoing, a taking-back of all the wounding words and mad revenges.

After I don't know how long I asked him how he was getting on at home. He breathed deeply and lowered his eyes, in disappointment and resignation. His shoulders dropped a little and his spine bent to a desultory curve as he found his years again. Grand, he said. All they do these days is watch telly. And give out about the rain. They don't let on anything is different. They act like I've been there all along. And he squinted up his features for a second, the way he always used to do after telling a story, as though to reinforce the truth of it, and I laughed at the sight of his squint and he said, What? and he smiled, and I smiled back. And there we were, just yesterday evening, out there in the hall, talking to each other, and smiling, while the sun dropped and the moon rose and the lawnmowers one by one fell silent.

They got a bit antsy the day you went gaga inside in town all right.

What?

The day you were inside in town with the little knacker one and started roaring at Elsie Brien and Mamie Graney and them. About the prostitutes. Fuck it like, Melody. That was bad form. Elsie and Mamie came down all guns blazing. Said they were only passing along what was being said, they knew there was no truth in it, that one was only ever trouble, but they had to tell what was being said.

Don't say knacker. She's a Traveller.

Are you teaching her to read as well?

I was. She's gone off somewhere.

Do you need money?

Why, do you have some?

I got a rake of tax back. I overpaid the cunts the year we went wallop. Imagine.

And he talked on about the taxman and how he was starting up again, and he was only going doing the smallest of jobs and was going paying the providers cash as he went, and how Ignatius Farrell was going around like the devil bit his bollix off since I named him inside in town, and how it was funny being away from me even though he knows the way it was wasn't right, not for years had it been right, and we may as well have been strangers but still, and he talked on saying nothing much, and we were sitting by now at the kitchen table, and at last he came to silence and he waited and so did I, and when he had the words worked up he said: Would you not get rid of it?

And there were tears suddenly falling from his eyes and he'd reached towards me but I had moved back away from him and he was saying, We could go away, we could go anywhere, there's the world of work in Canada, and they're mad looking for chippies and sparks, and we could go somewhere up the north, where there's snow the whole year, you love snow, Melody, and no fucker there would know one thing about us, and we could leave our battles here behind and start again.

Okay, I said to him. So, if I get rid of this baby you'll take me back, and we can go live somewhere else?

Yes, he said, and he laid his hands palms up before me.

But I left them empty there and said: Anywhere? We can live anywhere?

Yes, he said again, and still his proffered palms awaited mine.

What if I sold the house and bought a mobile home and applied for a berth on the halting site on the Ashdown Road? Would you live there with me?

And he looked in my eyes and saw that all that was there for him was pity, and he laughed gently, and he closed his eyes to dam a fresh river of tears, and he balled his open hands to fists, and he pressed the fists to the sides of his head, and he stood suddenly so that his chair fell back, and he said, What the *fuck* is it with you and knackers? YOU AND YOUR FUCKING KNACKERS!

And he turned and bent and picked up the fallen chair by its back and he swung it over his head and down, and the legs of it snapped and splintered across the floor. And I closed my eyes and held my breath, and gripped the table edges tight, and moments later he was gone, and all he left behind him was an echo of invective, ringing in my ears and fading to silence. And I thought for a second or two about calling him back, and asking if he'd like to go to bed.

Week Twenty-six

BECAUSE A TERRIBLE need has come over me, a burning, scorching want. It's not that warm outside tonight, there's a smell of rain in the air, but I have the bedroom window open and I'm covered in sweat and even the coolness of the breeze is adding to it, stroking my naked skin, stoking this imposturous flame. Every time I close my eyes I see Martin Toppy, his wide, suntanned shoulders, his V-shaped torso, his arms either side of me, his blue blazing eyes, his voice whispering, Miss, oh, miss, I love you. I see Pat, too, seventeen-year-old Pat, whiter and ropier than Martin Toppy but no less beautiful, his eyes shut tight with the effort of holding back, to please me, to make sure I knew he was a man, and could satisfy me, his woman, his girl.

There's a lad that holds a STOP sign at the roadworks on the bypass. He winked at me one day when I was at the front of the queue, and he held my eye and smiled. I saw him running on the Long Hill one evening, in a singlet and shorts. He has long, muscular legs. I woke from a dream where I slowed beside him as he ran, and stopped when he noticed me, and he stood sweating on the path across a narrow grass strip from the road, heaving breaths in and out, and I leant across and opened the passenger door, and he got in, and I tried to slip back into the dream when I woke drenched from it, but instead I dreamt of a wooden ship, tossed on a black sea, its hold packed tight with children and their mothers, their fathers and husbands lying flat on the pitching deck, whispering prayers to an absent God, and I woke again and there was a taste of salt on the breeze that touched my face from the open window, and I was coverless in the dark, and I breathed in and breathed out and lay still.

I stopped on the road near Borrisokane to get sick. I stood in a gateway, watched by a long-lashed cow, until I heaved and moaned and my moan turned half to a scream and the cow ran away in fright, shitting as she went. I leant back against the bonnet of my car and wiped vomit from my chin and tears from my eyes and watched a gap of blue as it was closed by clouds, and the sky darkened and the air cooled around me and a mist of rain wetted my forehead, and I rested against the car and gave consideration to turning and going home, and trusting in my instinct that my baby's limbs were forming, his heart beating strong. Why look in at him? Millions of years of babies were born with no scans or ultrasounds having checked their progress, and here we all are. But I drove on anyway, across the clanking bridge in Portumna, and along the narrow, snaking road north, and through the wide gates of the cold granite building at the edge of Ballinasloe, and I gave them a name, and a PPS number, and an address, and I gave them a father's name too, and I laid my left hand flat against the desk so my wedding ring could be seen and noted, and the solitaire below it that Pat had paid for with his first three months' wages as a qualified electrician.

He didn't drink or smoke a cigarette those whole three months, and cycled to the sites to save on fuel; he barely ate. And he knelt and held it out before me by a fountain in the gardens of Birr Castle, and I was surprised even though I'd known he was buying it, because we'd agreed ages before that we were getting engaged, and had fought dozens of fights about the mechanics of it, and still he said, Will you marry me? and I looked into his uncertain eyes and said, Yes, and I don't remember smiling, or him smiling, and his hand shook a bit as he put the ring on my finger and he said that we could change it, and I'd wanted a cluster on a band and not a solitaire, but I thought of him in the shop, in the small room where they take men to look at trays of rings held out by pretty girls in tight blouses and tighter skirts, and how red he would have been, and unsure, and my anger rose as quickly as my shame, and they battled there behind my eyes as he watched, and hardly breathed, and I said, No, love, it's perfect, and it was.

I didn't tell them at the hospital about my miscarriages, because I couldn't, and anyway all I want is to be told what I already know, and the plump nurse smiled and asked for my date of birth and I asked her why she wanted that and she smiled again and her eyeballs bounced left and right in mock wonder and she wrote the date of birth I gave her onto her form in a slow, careful cursive that riled me to watch it, and she called me dear, though she was five years younger than me at least, and she sent me through a door marked ULTRASOUND WAITING ROOM, and I sat in a circle of a dozen other women and a handful of comfortless men, who, not knowing where their eyes should rest, had clamped them to their iPhone screens, around a table of dog-eared magazines. When finally my turn came the technician was young and blonde and impossibly beautiful, and a tear escaped my eye when the heartbeat boomed through her tiny amplifier, and she put her hand on mine and smiled and told me that everything looked and sounded perfect, and she printed off a row of photos and handed them to me, of shapes made of variations of light and dark, and I could hardly bear to look at them, and I heard an echo of cries that were never heard, and I wondered how much pain they had felt, my other babies, as they ebbed away.

The plump nurse called me as I walked back past her station and asked me if I wouldn't mind waiting a minute just to see the doctor for a quick chat, and I nodded because my mouth was dry and I didn't trust my voice, and after a few minutes she brought me to a room that was bare save for a small desk and two chairs and a line of books set on a single shelf the length of one wall. A tall, dark-skinned man stood reading from a chart, and his eyes when he looked up were brown and hooded, by tiredness, I think, and something else, and I found myself staring for too long in silence at his face, the straight line of his jaw, the wave in his jet-black hair, the crease in the centre of his chin, the straightness and the whiteness of his teeth. My dream floated back to the front of my mind, I don't know why, of the storm-tossed boat and the women and children huddled in terror and the flattened, praying men. He seemed as unsure as me at first, and then he smiled and asked me the same questions the nurse had about when I'd had my last period, and he asked if I smoked or had ever had high blood pressure, and he spoke on in a reassuring tone, though I'm not sure exactly what he said, because unbidden thoughts had taken over my mind, of my third miscarriage, known only to Pat, that was like a very heavy period, but I had known without question or doubt that my body had rid itself of something not right, unviable, chanceless, and Pat had looked at the blood on my nightdress, and the tears on my face, and he had turned away and stood looking out the bedroom window at the rain. A few months later he had stood in the same spot, facing me, naked save for a bandage where the cut was made, saying, I had to, Melody, I had to. So it can never happen again.

This is how I justify my sin. That there was nothing else that I could do. That Pat had had himself vasectomized to punish his body for the pain it had caused, to punish himself, to save me, to punish me. That life will change its shape and form to suit its own propagation, that flesh is bound to beget flesh, that I was a blind vessel. That something passed unspoken between Martin Toppy and me, something from outside of us, that we both felt and that we didn't need to understand, because it wasn't our business to know the workings of Nature and Fate. That the pressure that built from week to week behind our dam of embarrassment and propriety was a blessed thing. Blessed by what or whom we didn't know, and didn't need to know, and we felt it there, the up to then occluded force, in the heat on each other's lips when finally the dam was broken in my kitchen and everything came cascading down and covered us, and we were senseless and helpless, drowning, and our actions were the same as the struggles of drowning people for air. This is how I justify my sin.

But others would say: You dirty bitch. Don't dress it up. You took a lad barely half your age and used him, you fucking rode him, because you couldn't deny yourself. You couldn't just be decent. You sat too close to him at his lessons, and left your hand on him too long as you pretended to be encouraging him and praising him; you wore a blouse that'd water the eye of a blind man and a skirt that showed more than a boy should be shown whose father is paying you to teach him to read and write, and trusting you to hold up your end of the bargain, and you changed from your tracksuit in the minutes after Pat left for training and before Martin arrived, and you took care about your underwear, and the perfume you dabbed on the pulse at your neck, and that is evidence enough to convict you, for your wrongs were all voluntary acts, and all acts done with criminal intent and with malice aforethought. You tormented that boy, and spoke soft to him, and pushed yourself against him, and you breathed on the flame of his passion until it couldn't be controlled. What boy of seventeen wouldn't go mad for a woman like you? A woman divorced from decency, without restraint. An old boiler in middling nick, gagging for it. A mad, horny bitch.

Week Twenty-seven

BREEDIE FLYNN WAS put sitting beside me on her first day in our school. We were in fourth class and she started two weeks into the term. Her family had moved back from Dublin, where her father was something in a bank. She told me in a strange, pretty accent that she liked my Care Bears pencil case, and she sniggered softly. She was taller than me, and she was beautiful, and her brown hair hung down across her face. Already she had bumps and redness on her cheeks.

A few minutes later, she turned suddenly to me and whispered: You know *bears* don't really *care*, don't you? And I said nothing back, because there was nothing to say to that, so stunned was I by all the things about her that were not me. No, they fucking don't. They fucking eat people, so they do. And then they shit them out all over the woods. So don't be thinking those furry fuckers are your friends. They'd eat you in a heartbeat and shit you out. All they do is eat and shit. Fucking bears. I hate them. And then she

smiled and said she was sorry and told me she was just cross about
having to live in this shithole and she had Care Bears at home herself and did I want to come and see them, and I said I did.

I called to Daddy to tell him about the scan. I told him the child
is fine, and asked did he want to see the pictures from the ultrasound and he said he did, and he rummaged among the envelopes
and flyers and knick-knacks on the mantelpiece for his glasses,
and he put them on almost ceremoniously, and he took the small
rectangular sheet of images from me, and he held it out from
himself in hands that trembled slightly, and he was silent a long
while before he said, Oh. Lord save us. Isn't it a sight altogether
what they're able to do? And is it a little boy or girl? And I wondered
at myself. How I could embarrass my father this way.

When the doorbell went today I saw the shape of Pat through the
frosted side-glass and I hesitated in the hall. I couldn't have borne
another scene of tears and temper. But it was his father, standing
in the same crooked, long-limbed way, head bowed like his son.
He had a roll-up on the go when I opened the door and the stench
of it burnt in my nostrils and settled in the back of my throat. He
flicked it away into my lawn of wild grass and dandelions like a
pub-door smoker about to turn back to the darkness. The gesture
didn't suit him, or didn't suit my image of him, cardiganed and
slippered in his soft-carpeted living room, welcoming and kind-
eyed like my own father. His clothes seemed wrong: jeans and a
checked shirt and a pair of bright white runners, jarring somehow
in their jauntiness against the creases on his face, his weary eyes.
Hello, Paddy, I said, as though I'd been expecting him. He shifted
his weight from foot to foot and still he hadn't met my eye, and
the smoke of his discarded fag was wisping straight skyward in the
breezeless air. The air seemed cold about him and the angles of

him seemed sharply defined; all his pleasantness was absent, his fatherly softness. At last he lifted his face and asked could he come in a minute. I felt like saying, No, Paddy, you can't. I don't have anything to say, and I don't think you have anything I want to hear. But I stood back and held the door open and I saw that there was a thick envelope in his hand, and he walked into the kitchen and stood at the far end of the table so that he was haloed by morning sun, and I was glad that the strange edges of him were obscured.

Will you have a cup of tea, Paddy? I said, and the words were out before I knew they were coming.

I won't, he said. Gor, I won't. And his words were certain and clipped. Here was a Paddy I'd never met before, not even the day he'd come for Pat's things. He laid his envelope down on the table and he pointed at it. That's a thousand euros, he said. And I can send you on a thousand more. Send me on? To Salthill, in Galway. A friend of mine has a house over there empty and he said you can have it for a year at least. Maybe more, depending how he finds you. Paddy kept his eyes on his enveloped wad and his hands on the back of a chair. His voice lowered a little and a tremble entered it, and I felt sad, suddenly, for this man I'd known half my life but had never really known. I could hear Agnes coaching him, counting the notes and re-counting them, mourning them, telling him not to come back inside that door till it was sorted and that one was gone from this town.

He looked at me at last and his eyes were glistening. Do you know at all the damage you have done? And I let my silence serve as answer. My boy's at home and he only a shell. The things you done. The things you said he done. I don't want to know about any of it. All I know is what I see with my own eyes and what I see with my own eyes is my boy at home curled up in a ball and you standing here with a bastard inside in you by some other fella and you having my family's good name destroyed going round telling lies and the only saving grace is the whole town knows you're a lunatic the same way your mother was, God rest her and God forgive me. Now, in the name of Jesus and all the saints of Heaven and for the love of Our Lady, will you, please, take this, and go on away out of it? I'll drive you myself if you're not able. I'd pull a barrow behind me and walk it, just to have you gone, the way Pat can forget about you. You'll sell this house easy, and the few bob there and what I'll send you on will see you right till then, and Lord knows the state is only mad to hand out money to ones like you. The address is inside in the envelope, and a key. All you need do is ring the ESB once you get there and they'll turn the power back on. It's fully furnished, and there's a view of the bay, and the promenade only steps away. And we'll go in as far as Walshes the solicitors, Pat and myself, and get the ball rolling legal-wise, and we'll see about ending all this for good and glory, and putting my boy back together. He could have a good life yet.

Oh, could he? I said. Isn't it well for him? Go on away, Paddy, and take that envelope with you. And I pointed to the corner by the stove and said, And you can take the bits of that chair that your precious Pat fucking smashed across the floor here a few weeks ago while you're at it. And I closed my eyes and breathed deep, and steadied myself against the worktop, and when I opened them the window bay was empty and the front door was clicking closed.

My baby is fattening now, and he has eyelashes, and I know they're long and dark, and he opens and closes his eyes. I stand in the bay window and hold up my top, so he's bathed in a shaft of light, and imagine him looking in wonder at it, and blinking at it, and reaching his little hand out to it. I lie along the couch and softly sing, a stupid song I only half remember. I feel him gently bumping at the walls that keep him in, stretching and yawning and settling to wait.

Week Twenty-eight

IT'S A FEW days now since Paddy came. The envelope is still on the table. I haven't touched it yet, and hope I'll never have to. Pat will come again, surely, and when he does I'll make him take it away with him. I texted him that night, and said, I'M GOING NOWHERE, and he sent back a question mark, and then he rang, but I hadn't the heart for the fight so I turned my phone off and it's been off since.

My father came this morning and surveyed my garden, and the weeds that line the joins of the concrete flags in the back yard, and he sat a while at the kitchen table and I said, You're looking better than you were, less stiff, and he said, Yerra, I was never too bad, but I went as far as Croom the way Dr Laurence said I should for that auld shot of stuff, you know, the what-do-you-call-it, the cortisone, I think it's called. I don't like to get it, to be honest. It couldn't be right. But I do be able to get a lot of jobs done after it I wouldn't have been able for otherwise.

And that's as much as my father ever revealed to me about his health, about the pains that rule him now, and all I said back was, Oh, good, Dad, I'm glad.

So he strimmed down the jungle in my front garden and raked the cuttings to a tidy pile, and mowed the clipped tufts to a crew-cut, and I saw him straighten slowly with his two hands to the small of his back, and his eyes were closed and his teeth were bared, for all his talk about the shots that took away his stiffness and his pain. And a woman watched him from across the road as she tended her own garden, and he waved at her and she waved back, and they exchanged some words about the day, and whether they'd escape the rain. And I stood with my hands crossed on my belly, feeling the warmth that courses there, the speeding blood.

I drove the long way round to Daddy's yesterday. I slowed and stopped at the halting site entrance and studied the windows and door of Mary's caravan, and saw nothing there had changed, but the branches on the trellis had grown out and soon would meet across her door, and early roses bloomed pink and orange, and I wondered what nourished their roots in the scrubby patch of earth either side of Mary's steps. Maybe someone now and then put horse manure there, Mary's father, or one of the older boys. Was she set completely apart?

I long to see her, and sit with her, and watch her eyes as they travel across the pages of a children's book, and her lips as they form the words, and her eyes as they search mine for approval.

The sentry leant and yawned against the concrete gatepost, and the small boys sparred and darted still, and a dappled pony stood and chewed and watched them, a rope halter dangling from its neck and tied to nothing. Vans attended every bay but Mary's and her family's, and I felt a prickling all across my fingertips and toes, and knew my heart had skipped a beat, and then I felt it palpitate, and I wondered how my body knew to do these things, how it was so certain how I felt when I wasn't sure I knew myself. Mary Crothery makes me calm, that's all I really know. The sentry noticed me at last and he raised a meaty arm in salute and I nodded and smiled and drove away. Daddy wasn't home so I waited in my car and cried, and wondered who the tears were for. Breedie Flynn, and Mary Crothery, and my mother, and my father, and Pat. And myself, most of all.

The skies are dark and the air is heavy and still. My skin is coated in sweat. In the supermarket today I stopped before a freezer of pizzas and put my basket on the floor and slid the glass top of the cabinet open. I stood in the blessed cool air that wafted from it and closed my eyes, and when I opened them there was an old woman shuffling bent-backed towards me and she cocked her crone face at my growing bump and she said, They don't know darkness, you know. Angels light their way for them. And her face creased to a smile and she straightened and was gone.

Another morning. There's a smell of rain. That longing came on me again last night and I lay as still as I could and thought about other things, and I walked the house in the hours before dawn nearly naked, to use my muscles, to stretch them out, to see could I make them weary. I held my phone in my hand and wrote text after text to Pat, deleting them all before sending them, asking him to call over. I felt again the way I felt in college when I came off the pill because I couldn't afford it, and neither could Pat, and he never had a condom, and we'd be in my narrow bed, and I'd want him to stay going, and I'd weigh the moment against my life beyond the moment, and the heat would blind me and the moment would triumph, and we'd give days and weeks to worry till my period came. What if I let these moments triumph now, and let Pat sneak like a teenager from his parents' house and walk through the still bright night and I'd let him in, and let him in, and his heart would be lifted in hope, and I'd have to break it down again once I'd finished with him? Could I do it? I didn't this time, but the next time, I don't know.

Week Twenty-nine

MARY CROTHERY CAME back today. Oh, thank God, I said, when
I saw her at my door.

What? she said back, and looked at me with her top lip dragged
across and curled in mock derision.

Where were you? I asked, and heard crossness in my voice.

Mind your own fuckin business, she said, and laughed at the
shock on my face, and looked back at my trim lawn and said,
Who done that for you?

My father, I told her and she said, Isn't he a great man? If I
done what you done my father would of killen me. He's a quiet
man, your father. How old is he?

He'll be seventy-two this Christmas, I said, and she told me her
father was up around forty, there was no one full sure, and he had
a woeful gut on him but still and all was stronger than any man of
twenty and was able for anyone, and put the fear of God in men,
and she raised a hand to her face and was crying suddenly, and her

thin shoulders were shuddering beneath her denim jacket, and tears were mingling with the glitter on her skin-tight jeans, and I stood looking at her and she turned to leave, but something in my voice must have given away my desperation for her to stay.

Please, I said, and grabbed her hand.

She looked at me and squinted and sniffed and said, You're not going lesbian on me, miss, are you?

There'd been a fight at the wedding. The Folans were related to the groom, the Crotherys to the bride. Mary hadn't been there: she was left in a house owned by her mother's cousin, and had been allowed only to help her sisters with their outfits and their makeup and their fake tans. You should of seen them, miss, my little Margaret especially, Lord, she was beautiful, a rale spangly top all sequins down along in a V to her belly button and the skirt was perfect with it and the legs of her are gone so long you wouldn't believe, and it was nearly like it used to be before the trouble, and my heart nearly split in two when they all went off without me again.

But there was war broke out at the reception. Mommy had an offer ready for the Folans for peace, and there was a fair-play family asked to come and all, the way there'd be no fighting while the offers was been made, and she had Daddy told he was to ask the Folans would they take a ball of money, I don't know how much, and we'd leave them have our tarmacaddanin rights all around places we always had them for years and years, and me and Buzzy's divorce would be clane and quick and everything would be set back nearly to the way it was, and they said, No. There'd be no forgiveness. And one of them told Daddy he sent over used goods to Buzzy and that'd never be forgot, and Daddy busted the sayer of that across the head with a cider bottle and that was that, all hell broke loose and the shades arrived, and there was a good lot took away in paddy-wagons and a good lot more took away in ambulances, and we ran for the ferry next morning. And Mommy the whole way home blamed me. This is your doing, she kept saying and saying, this is your doing. And my daddy told her shut up after a good while cause he was sick I'd say of listening to her, and he said, She can't help the way she is, God made her barren, and that's it, that's it now, and there's to be no more about it, and Mommy only looked at me like I was a thistle in a bed of flowers, but she knew not to stay going with my daddy the way he was then, and one side of his face all swole up where he'd a right dig got off of a Folan, and she moved my sisters and my brother away from me to a different part of the boat but Daddy stayed sitting beside me and told me about the fight and the man he brained with the bottle over insulting me and I was never happier in a long, long time than I was then, and the rocking of the boat didn't frighten me as much.

So now there's been a fight there'll be a feud. Hot blood runs to bad blood. And none of it Mary's fault, nor Buzzy's, all of it down to a foul alignment and crossing of their stars. And every day I wait to hear the news, and none ever comes, but her parents are on high alert, and there's a half a dozen cousins posted now across the gate where before my sleepy sentry stood alone, and there's talk of a fair fight to settle things, but that's a long way down the road yet. There'll be skirmishes first, it seems, and allies to both sides will be mobilized. I drive every day to the site to collect her, and no Folan, as mad as they are, would be foolish enough to attack a settled person's car, a country person's car. Mommy stands some days behind the rank of freckled watchmen, her stout arms folded on her chest, and watches me as I wait, and nods as I leave, and I try ever harder to make Mary literate, to justify myself in Mommy's eyes, because she has some kind of power that makes me want to please her. We do our ABCs and read Dr Seuss and Enid Blyton and some books I borrowed from the library aimed at helping adults who got left behind. And Mary tucks her hands between her legs and hunches down low to the pages and she tries and tries. And sometimes I hear Breedie when she says my name.

Breedie thought my mother was a queen, or a kind of aristocrat at least. When she came to our house to watch telly or listen to music or just to sit on the swings and talk delicious nonsense, she always asked where my mother was, and looked disappointed if she was in her room, as she often was, with the curtains closed, lying down. My mother always spoke pointedly to Breedie, and asked her how she was, and how her parents were, and offered her biscuits or crisps, and Breedie always refused, and my mother would say, That's it, keep your figure, and she'd smile at Breedie, and leave the offered treats in front of me, and I'd wonder as I ate them what good a figure was, and I'd wonder exactly what a figure was meant to be, and I'd look down at my childish body, short-legged and chubby, and I'd look at Breedie's long bare arms, and long legs, and graceful neck, and her pale skin and wide blue eyes, and I'd feel a fizzing mixture of admiration and love and terrible envy, that she could make my mother smile and wish she had a daughter like a swan.

And all the parts of Breedie that were tense in her own house were relaxed in ours: her shoulders and her back and her eyes, and she laughed longer and more loudly than she did there. My mother for all her haughtiness never minded us having fun. She'd stand sometimes at the kitchen sink smoking while we played, smiling, I think, though I never looked long enough to be certain. And one sunny day I looked from the end of the garden and saw my father there through the window and they were facing each other and they kissed each other on the lips for a moment before drawing apart and I felt a kind of happiness I hadn't thought was possible. But that only happened the once.

Week Thirty

A BRICK CAME through my window late last night. I woke with the crash and thought it was a dream, and fell back to sleep, and woke again in the early morning, and walked in the half-light around the house as I do now all the time, to ease the stiffness in my legs and back. Passing the front room I saw the glass and the billowing curtain, and the splatters of rain on the couch, and the brick that sat all innocent on the floor in a puddle of shards. There was something written on the brick, in Tipp-Ex or white paint, but I couldn't make it out by the streetlamp and the dawn light, and I couldn't move from where I was, even to flick the light switch, and minutes passed, I'd say, before I stirred and took my hand down from my mouth and stepped slowly into the room. I stood well back and leant forward and saw the word SLAG printed on the top side, and DIE SLUT on the long side and CUNT on the short side, and the other sides I couldn't see, nor did I want to. And my first thought was this, and maybe this means I'm mad:

There should be a comma between DIE and SLUT. Vocative case, I tutted in my crazy head.

Jim Gildea came to my door and my first words to him were: I thought you were retired.

And he said, So did I, and kind of smiled. There was a girl behind him swallowed by a luminous jacket, and her garda hat seemed too big for her head, and her flat, dark eyes were going up and down me and in past me to the hallway, and Jim said, This is Carol, and corrected himself a moment later: Garda Morris. She's new, he said, and he smiled at me, a proper smile this time, and asked could he come in. And we stood, the three of us, just inside the living-room doorway, looking at the brick and the broken glass, and no one spoke for long moments until Jim said, What does it say on it?

And the way he emphasized *on* made him sound so like my father that for a second I forgot myself and held on to his arm, and I felt my face contorting as I said: Slag. It says, Slag, and it says, Die, slut, and it says, Cunt.

Oh, Jim said. I see, faith.

Jesus, Garda Morris said, and leant out around Jim's belly to look at me, up and down and up and down again.

Would you mind not looking me up and down? I said to her. That's twice you've done it now. Shouldn't you be inspecting the brick, not me? She pursed her lips and turned away, and Jim huffed a little laugh through his nose and for a second I was sure he was going to say something, like Go on away out now, the two of ye, and play in the yard awhile and I'll sort this out, but he just said, Ah, now. Right. Come on and we'll have a cup of tea. Draw back the curtains fully there, Carol, the way they won't be flapping. And he looked down at me and winked and said: Like some of the mouths around here. And he put his big hand on my elbow as we processed down the hallway to the kitchen.

It's a wonder they didn't put it through your car window, Jim said. Would have been easier. They were bould, whoever they were. They'd have had to stand inside in your garden. Carol and myself will clean up the glass for you for fear you'd wound yourself, and I'll take away the brick with me, but you know yourself now.

Know what, Jim?

Yerra, how these things go. Everyone knows and no one knows who does these things. Lads do be on bicycles doing devilment, creeping around all night. The amount of houses around here now that was never here before it's hard keep track of all the bowsies. Someone was put up to this now for a dare or something like that, you can be assured. Heard a bit of a story and made a right drama out of it.

And Jim looked up at the tops of my kitchen cabinets and down at the unswept floor and over at the dishes in the sink and asked how was I in myself, was I getting along all right, was I on my own the whole time, and I said, Yes, I'm on my own the whole time, I'm fucking left here, Jim, at the mercy of fucking . . . FUCKERS!

And I wondered at my own ineloquence, and Carol made a snorting, choking sound and spat some tea back into her mug, and Jim just smiled ruefully and said, Ah, now. Would you not go out and stay with your father for a while? I see him nearly every morning walking in the road to Mass. He's a grand man, your father. I'd say he'd love the company.

Oh, just get the fuck out, I said, and took his mug from his hand, and Carol started saying something in a sharp, tinny voice, and Jim cut her with a look and went searching for his hat, and he stopped and turned to me, and he leant down towards me as if he was about to say something of great importance, and he laid one hand softly on my arm, and he said: Had I my hat on me when you answered the door?

*

So the glass and the brick were taken away, and someone came and replaced the broken pane. And I probably should have told Jim and his protégée about Ignatius Farrell, because it was probably him, but I never did. What would I have said? He came here one evening not long ago with a face of murder on him and he slammed my door open and I think maybe he was going to beat me up, or rape me, or both? He didn't threaten me. He asked me what I was saying about him. He called me a cunt. He assumed a threatening aspect. Not enough to go on, Jim would have said. I'll call down to him for a chat, Jim would have said. A chat about fucking hurling, probably, I would have said. And there'd have been even more hurt and confusion in poor Jim's eyes, and his hat would never have been found.

Mary Crothery came while the glazier was still here. I told her what had happened, though I hadn't meant to. Is a slag and a slut the same thing? she asked.

I suppose, I said, more or less.

I wouldn't be fond of the *die* bit, though, miss. It's never good to have people wanting to take your life from you. We were camped one time in a farmer's field, and we had the man's permission got and all, I think Daddy guv him money and the man was woeful hard on the drink and didn't give one shit who was camped on his land once he had enough for a few days on the batter, and someone come in the night and fired two shots from a shotgun in through the side of Daddy's Transit, but no one was in it when they done it because it was late in the night, and no one got a scratch bar my daddy, and that was only where he fell onto his hands and knees at the wagon door thanking God there was none of us hurt. My brother and sisters was all only very small that time, and I was still Mommy's favourite girl and she nearly squez the life out of me.

*

There's a pint and a half of fluid around my baby now. It doesn't seem enough. I like the thought of him floating, suspended, weightless. But he weighs around three pounds now and our worlds have the same pull of gravity. My feet seem flat and huge; my shoes pinch. I'm barefoot most of the day. I find myself sitting still with my eyes closed, humming to him, listening for a response. I feel him listening. I felt him push his hand against my hand. I know what has to happen now, and I think I always did. The story was there all along, in the wheeling stars, in its entirety, the parts already told and all the parts to come, Brailled in dots of light against the black.

Week Thirty-one

I DIDN'T TELL Daddy about the brick. Bad enough him knowing what he knows. Bad enough him petting me and minding me and he in pain down to his bones. Bad enough to think of him making another appointment to go to the orthopaedic hospital in Croom through Dr Laurence, and apologizing for being a nuisance as Dr Laurence wrote his longhand note, and panicking over where his medical card was, and fretting over the drive on the motorway, and gripping the wheel tighter as lorries passed him for fear that all the wind of them would blow him from his course, and squinting up at road signs for his exit, and sitting in a waiting room and making small-talk about the weather with who-ever was facing him there, and humming to himself in feigned nonchalance, and looking out the window at the trees, and red-dening in the rooms as he undresses to be examined and considered and injected, and nodding his understanding at words he doesn't understand, and writing out his cheque for a bored secretary with a shaking hand, apologizing all the while for being so slow, for holding her up, for keeping her from her work. As if there's any work more important for her than watching old men writing cheques, making sure they don't forget to sign them.

I asked him could I stay with him for a while, and I saw him look at my middle before he replied and some strange expression flashed cold across his eyes for less than a second and then was gone. Something he couldn't help, I'd say, believing as he does, loving his mother church as he does, with such firmness, such quiet, unthinking fervour. That I stopped going to Mass at fourteen was hard enough to take for him; that Pat and I lay together before we were married was harder again; that he'd seen us with his two eyes in bed together; that I'm separated now and pregnant by a man not my husband, that the child inside me is the product of a mortal sin, must cause him pain that I could never fully know. And still I come and ask him to protect me, and let me sleep again in my childhood bed, and wait for him to tell me things are perfect, and lay his lovely hand on my cheek, and kiss the top of my bowed head.

He was standing and I was sitting, and he rubbed his hands together and said, Yes, love, of course you can, you can stay for ever if you want. And suddenly my tears came on again, and I tried to stanch them but I couldn't, and he must be sick by now of petting me, and saying things like: Ah, now, love, come on now, it'll be all right, everything will work itself out in the end.

Mary Crothery said she thinks they're going on the road. Something clenched itself inside me, and released, and clenched again, and I felt the inside of my mouth turn dry, and I couldn't answer her. They have to move around the way they won't be sitting ducks for the Folans, or the Windrums, who are on the Folans' side, or the Dodrells or the Cantys or the Stokeses. You'll miss me, miss, I'd say, she said. I'll miss you, too. We're the same as wan another, you and me, she said, just as she had the second time we met, when she seemed to see inside me to my soul, and to know I'd done things of which I was ashamed, and to know I was cast out the way she was. To know I was pregnant, when no sign of this existed. Mary says she has a taste of a vision. I love to hear her say that, the matter-of-factness of it; the unquestioning acceptance of things that can never be seen or grasped or known. I love the way she speaks my name sometimes instead of calling me miss, and I hear Breedie, and I'm fairly sure now that it is Breedie, and I think that maybe she forgives me, though I can't imagine ever forgiving myself. I can't imagine my days without her now.

Mary has her days free now, while councils of war are being held, once she has the wagons cleaned and breakfasts and lunches made. She hasn't to be back till supper time. She helped me bring some of my things to Daddy's. Then we drove to Limerick because she couldn't concentrate on her words, because it was different, she said, being in a strange house, and she'd have to get used to it, and she felt terrible guilty, she said, that my father left his own kitchen on her account. I suggested we go shopping for maternity gear because all my jeans and skirts were gone too tight, and she talked the whole journey, a tide with no ebb, of words and questions and jokes and jibes, and she gave two fingers to a speed van we passed near Birdhill, and she laughed and said, You'll get done now for that, not me, making rude signs in public, there'll be a photo took of it, and you'll be held responsible for the *behaviyaaaw of yaw passengeaaaw* and I'll be long gone, laughing back at you. Will you miss me, miss? Will you? And I didn't answer her; I let her rile me so I wouldn't start to cry. And she fell silent as we edged through the heavy midday traffic into the city and after a while she said: I'll have to go away on the road, miss, but I'll be back again as sure as God. Don't abandon me, sure you won't? Promise me you won't abandon me.

And I promised, and when I looked across at her she had her eyes closed and her hands clasped together in her lap and her lips were moving as though in prayer.

A security guard followed us around the shop. Watch your man behind, Mary said to me. I have him well clocked the very same as he thinks he has me clocked. And before I could ask her what she meant she turned from the rack of maternity dresses we'd been looking at and said in a loud voice, Are you in love with me? And she waited patiently for the security guard's reply, but none came. He stood in the aisle and looked at her and his expression was set in mock boredom and didn't change. Are you in love with me, fine sir? The way you can't take your eyes off of me? Will we go way and get married, will we? And have grand little security guard children?

And a group of meaty women stopped to watch the drama, and Mary turned to them and back to the security guard and said, More in your line keep an eye on that fuckin herd of buffaloes before they go on a stampede around the place.

And the women in unison dropped their jaws in indignation, and one of them said, Fuck you, you little bitch, and still the security guard stood his shaky ground, too embarrassed to back away and too thick to find words to defuse things, and Mary shouted on.

What is it about me? I haven't even a bag with me to put stuff into. Why do you think I'm a thief? I never done notten in here ever before. You never seen me before in all your days. And the guy still said nothing, just stood and fiddled with the buttons on the top of his walkie-talkie, and I stood uselessly beside my friend and I had no words to offer in support, and when she turned to me and said, All I'm doing is shopping with my friend, I still said nothing, just stood with a dress like a parachute in my hands, and I felt myself redden and I don't know why, but I think Mary took it as a sign that I was ashamed, and she said, You're a fine one, to be turning embarrassed, the fuckin scene you made last time we was in town, and she turned away from me and walked towards the escalator, jostling the stocky security guard as she went, so hard that he nearly fell, and he said something into his walkie-talkie, and I dropped my dress and crossed the aisle towards him and grabbed the walkie-talkie from his hand and threw it hard onto the floor. I'm getting really good at that trick. He cursed and bent to retrieve it, and it had come apart but was still crackling, and a voice from it was saying, She's heading for the door now, do you want me to stop her? Over. And I shouted from the top of the escalator towards the door, DON'T YOU FUCKING LAY A FINGER ON THAT GIRL, and Mary turned around and smiled and said, Ah, here, miss, we're some fuckin troublemakers, and we laughed as the door was held open for us and we sashayed out on to the street, us two.

As I drove home after dropping Mary I felt a tightening in my middle and a whisper of darting pain. My heart hammered and jumped and tiny constellations popped in and out of existence before my eyes. I pulled into the Co-op yard and breathed slowly in and out. I remembered something, something, about pre-term contractions, and I couldn't think what. I typed *pre-term* on my phone and it finished the phrase for me and I clicked on the first link and read about Braxton-Hicks, and I laughed and cried at the same time, and I thanked God through my snot and tears, as Packie Collins and his cat-faced wife watched me from the Co-op door. I put the car in reverse instead of first and nearly took out their diesel pump, and I smiled apologetically and waved at them as I drove away. I saw them in my mirror staring still.

Week Thirty-two

THEY CAME WITHOUT warning in the night. Two vans of them, and one of them levelled a gun at the sentries while others went to the Crotherys' tiny compound, and they went slashing and pounding in through the windows and doors with weapons of iron and bent and bladed steel and Mary's father was dragged from his bed by three or four of them and one attacker had his skull cracked open by her father's great fist and they clubbed him to subdue him and he was stretched along the ground in the centre of the camp and his kneecaps were smashed with a cudgel, and Mary was taken from her tiny wagon through her doorway of roses and punched and kicked without mercy and was slashed along her leg and face and arm and Mommy was suddenly upon the attackers and she had a shotgun in her hands and it was tucked into her shoulder and she shot the gunman at the gate with one barrel and he fell, and his weapon skittered away from him across the ground to the shadows, and he was peppered and holed but he was not dead, and she shot at the men who'd kneecapped her husband and slashed her daughter with the other barrel, and the shot pocked the ground at their feet, and they backed away with their weapons raised uselessly in the face of the bosomy dervish advancing on them, and the screams of Mary Crothery's mother were louder than the shots, My husband, my child, ye bastards, ye bastards, I'll kill ye all, and in the time it took her to break her shotgun to reload they were gone, and no sign of them was left but for blood and broken glass and bones.

I heard about it on the radio as Daddy cooked us breakfast. He always has the radio tuned to local news and turned up loud for fear he'd miss the announcement of the deaths. Whisht, he said, and turned it louder still, and gestured to me to listen. I ran to my car and drove up the Long Hill and down the Ashdown Road and nearly side-swiped a garda van and was stopped by a helmeted guard with ARMED RESPONSE UNIT on his vest and a vicious-looking gun cradled like a baby in his arms, and I asked who was hurt, was anyone dead, where was Mary Crothery, and he said he didn't know who Mary Crothery was, but there was no one dead as of the last half an hour, that the casualties were all gone to the Regional in Limerick, and I was to turn around and go back the way I came: the road was closed.

I met Mary Crothery's mother in the lobby of the hospital, red-faced and weeping at a table strewn with sweet wrappers and Styrofoam cups and puddles of spilt drinks, a half-circle around her of children and cousins and clan. What's your business here? she said, and her voice was low, her throat was hoarse. There's none of this anyone's business only ours. And she bared her teeth and the children quietened and looked at me, and Margaret said: She lost a load of blood. They slashed her open. She's in intensive care. On the second floor. And that's it. We don't know notten else. Our daddy mightn't ever walk again. And they all wailed together, and Mommy smacked her daughter on the back of her head, and said: Don't be tellin that wan notten.

I left them there, and went to find my friend, and Margaret must have been hardened to defiance by the slap she'd been given, because she followed me and told me at the door of the lift what had happened to her father and to Mary, what she'd seen from the window in the night.

They replaced her spilt blood with the blood of strangers. I offered mine and a nurse asked was I pregnant and I said, Yes, and she said, Sorry, pet. But we have plenty spare, more than we need for the moment. We can draw from her mam and her sisters if needs be. Blood will never go astray.

She was as white as her pillow and her hair was spread around her almost artfully, as though someone was setting up a shot of her, for a magazine cover or an advert. I wanted to touch her, just to feel the heat in her, to know for sure she hadn't slipped away, but I was allowed only a look in from the door, and only for seconds. I sat for hours today at the edge of the ICU on a plastic chair, and Mommy and the children trooped in past me now and again and were intercepted by a kindly matron each time and turned back, and they didn't speak to me until late in the evening, as they came for a last look, and Mommy stood beside me and said, Thank you. And before I could reply she'd walked away.

Today, Mary Crothery died. Like rain from a blue sky it came, a sudden unbroken screech from the machine that stood sentry at her side, a swish of nurse and doctor and a clipped litany of commands. I knelt in the corridor outside, my forehead against cold concrete, a desperate mendicant, my hands out, beseeching, to God. Please, I begged, please, please, give her back, give her back. I heard sounds and words from within, familiar only from television, and imagined her little body bucking hopelessly as they tried to relight the tiny flame inside her that had been extinguished.

I don't know if I pleaded aloud, but a woman with white hair was suddenly stooped beside me, her hand on my back, her breath on my face. Come on, pet, she said, you're going to hurt yourself, mind your little baby, sit up on a seat at least. And I saw then through my tears that I had the narrow corridor blocked; a middle-aged man in a shirt of brilliant white with epaulets of funereal black was waiting, half smiling, to push a trolley past me. I stood, and wobbled, and the white-haired lady put a steadying hand on my elbow, an arm around my waist. I didn't look back at the door to the ICU; I imagined frantic movement inside, or a terrible stillness as a doctor checked his watch and solemnly uttered an hour and a minute.

She led me away from Mary towards an open area ringed by curtained cubicles. She put me on a chair, implausibly positioned in the centre of the floor area, like an obdurate rock in a rushing stream of nurses and porters and broken people, parting unseeing around me. She knelt in front of me, her hand resting gently on mine. Her voice was soft and familiar. I tried to focus on her.

They don't go away, you know. They never really leave us. She paused, as though waiting for me to show that I understood. Is she your daughter? I shook my head. Your sister?

No, I said, she's my friend. And friend then seemed a word with no force, no meaning that wasn't vague or imprecise; it didn't have power enough in its utterance to fully explain what Mary Crothery was to me. And as I thought this I realized that I had done the one thing that Mary had made me promise not to do: I had abandoned her. I cast the comforting hand aside and almost knocked the kindly woman over as I rose and ran, back through the maelstrom of casualties and harried staff, down the narrow corridor towards where Mary lay, and a nurse put a hand out to stop me at the door, and when I looked past her I saw that Mary's eyes were open and the machine had returned to its steady, tinny marking of a sinus beat, and she was back.

She came back. She stabilized. Her little heart, bruised and broken, had relit itself. She'd been gone, oh, she'd been gone, but she came back, plucked from the void, and I think I heard her laughing as I screamed my thanks to God.

Week Thirty-three

A FEW WEEKS after Breedie Flynn was buried, between her maternal grandparents, in front of the ruins of the old church in Kilscannell cemetery, my father said he'd met her mother in the shop. She wants to know will you go up to their house, he said, and just have a chat with them. I suppose they might get some comfort out of talking to you, and having you around the place, seeing as you and Breedie were such great pals always. And my heart thumped so hard in fear my vision blurred. I'd stood among the cool girls at the funeral, and hadn't even thrown earth in the grave; I'd tried my best to merge and blend and fade away from sight. We'd lined the churchyard in our uniforms, formed a guard of honour as she left for her last drive, and there'd been skitting in among the sobs, and the skitting was the boys being hard and the sobs were all for drama and for show, because Breedie had had no real friends left by then. And I couldn't watch her coffin being carried to the hearse, and I couldn't meet her mother's eye, and my heart pounded and my blood felt cold in my veins as I listened to her father's eulogy, when he'd said his lovely angel was gone from him, and then he stopped and he couldn't carry on, and after a minute or so of silence he left the pulpit with his hand across his face and his shoulders shuddering violently and he nearly fell on the step down from the altar.

I walked along their gravel avenue, between the lines of swaying poplars, watching the sunlight dappled green along the stones, and when at last I had the courage to raise my face I saw that they were waiting at the door. Her father said something, but I wasn't close enough to hear, and her mother grabbed his arm and said through gritted teeth, You promised me, Alan, you promised me. And I walked on towards them, thinking: This is the least I deserve. And they sat me in at their kitchen table and offered me coffee or tea or juice or water and I said, Water, please, and they sat in front of me side by side and Breedie's mother said: What happened to our daughter in that school? And it didn't sound like a question: it sounded like a heading, a headline, from one of those newspapers that my mother called filthy rags when she found them in my father's van or in the shed where he used to sit and smoke and read sometimes. And I said nothing, just looked from one face to the other, and seeing only anger there, and nothing in the way of sympathy for me – why should there have been? – I panicked, and I bawled just like a child. Oh, for fuck's sake, Breedie Flynn's father said, and turned away to face his wife, and gestured with a turn of his hand that this was no good.

Breedie told me she didn't just love her father, she was in love with him. And she hated her mother because she kept them apart. She said she sometimes put her hand on his leg when they were driving and he'd put his hand on top of hers and they'd drive along like that in silence, and her father would take long ways round to stretch out their time together and he'd take his hand off hers only to change the gears. They didn't need to speak because they were tuned so completely to each other's thoughts, she said, and she just looked at him, the strong jutting bone of his jaw, the greenness of his eyes, the stubble he let grow just for her, because she said she liked it, and she knew her mother hated it because she often nagged him to shave, and she'd look at the curls in his dark-brown hair and she'd watch the way the changing light attached itself to his face and hair and unattached itself again, changing his aspect, and seeming at times to make him more handsome still, as if that was possible.

Breedie told me how her mother would get drunk sometimes and slobber all over him and try to kiss him on the lips in front of her and she'd feel sick, and she'd feel sorry for him, because she knew he hated it, and sometimes she'd hear them in the bedroom and her mother would be crying and saying, Don't you love me any more? Did you ever love me? And she'd lie in her bed watching the darkness in the hall through the cracked-open door, watching for a shape or shadow there that never came.

There'd been some mistake somewhere, Breedie said, or some crime had been committed somewhere else in time, by one or both of them, and this was their punishment: they'd been sent into this existence out of sync, to be tormented till they purged themselves of whatever sin it was that they had done.

And I listened rapt to all of this, and swore I'd never ever breathe a word, and I cried with her and shared in all her sorrows, manufactured and real, and I believed none of it and I believed all of it and I believed Breedie believed it and so it was as true as it needed to be. And I looked sometimes at her handsome father and thought I saw a darkness in behind his eyes, and a strange kind of hungry sadness.

And a day came when I chose others over her, and I abandoned her, and went off into the world without her, and laughed about her secrets and her livid pitted skin, and said nothing when the lads sprayed BREEDIE FLYNN RIDES HER DA in bright-green paint all over the handball alley wall, and Tipp-Exed it on noticeboards in every classroom of our school.

I couldn't tell her parents this. Someone sprayed across the hand-ball alley graffiti after a few days, and it was on the inside anyway, where we went to shift and smoke fags, and no one played handball there any more because there was an indoor complex in the village by then, and Breedie went from room to room every lunchtime with a blade and scraped the noticeboards clean. And maybe it was the same blade she used to open lines along her arms, and she'd stand sometimes across from me in physics and she'd roll her shirt-sleeve up and lay her forearm out along the lab table so I could see, and she wouldn't say a word to me, just watch my face for second after second as I looked at the perfectly straight diagonal lines of thin black crust fading to purple at the edges that she'd forged into her skin across the inside of her arm from her wrist almost up to her elbow, and she'd roll her shirtsleeve down again and walk away, back to Miss Greene's desk, because she had no partner. And still I didn't tell them all to stop, to leave her, even the day in our home-room when she stood and said, Please, Melody, please, and her tears fell down along her face, and the salt of them must have stung her as they passed along her red-raw skin.

And a day came when Breedie Flynn's mother looked out from an upstairs window, and saw her daughter, sitting cross-legged and perfectly still on the grassless ground beneath her childhood swing set, light-yellow flames folded fully around her. She had taken a plastic can of petrol and a Zippo lighter to the bottom of the back garden at her parents' house, and she had doused herself, and lit herself, and burnt away.

Week Thirty-four

SO I SAT that day in front of her parents and I looked down into my glass of water and tried not to cry again because I had no right to, and it had maddened her father, and her mother asked me over and over again what had happened, why Breedie and I had fallen out; they'd asked her time and again and she'd never tell them, and she never once had a bad word about me, and she just said, She has a boyfriend now and she spends all her time with him, and her boyfriend's crowd don't like me, they're jealous of me or something, but it's grand because I have other friends, in the debating society and all that, I'm fine, I'm fine, just leave me alone, and she'd lock her door behind her till they took away her key, and she'd leave her curtains closed all day at the weekends and never let the sunlight touch her face. They weren't blaming me in any way, her mother said; Breedie had been clinically depressed, and they knew how friendships faded in and out in teenage years anyway, and how the smallest falling out can magnify and seem at the time to be the end of the world; they'd been there themselves, they knew exactly how it was. And I looked up then and she was sort of smiling, and Breedie Flynn's father was looking at me so intensely that my stomach burnt and my heart hopped and stuttered in my chest, and the two of them were so beautiful, like film stars, like pictures of people, even with the rings of shadow round their eyes and the creases grief had cut into their faces. And some message was carried across the air between Breedie Flynn's father and me, something I couldn't decipher but kind of understood; some feeling I couldn't put a name to, anger mixed with something else, a sort of an acceptance of some hideous alien truth.

Go on home, love, Breedie's mother said. This isn't fair on you. You've had your share of loss as well. Breedie always said she didn't do enough for you, you know, the time your mother passed away. She always thought she let you down. And I think we did, you know, all of us. And I mumbled something back, like, Of course not, everyone was lovely, everyone was great, I'm sorry about Breedie, I'm so, so sorry, and Breedie Flynn's mother stood and so did I and we embraced each other awkwardly, and she walked me to the door and let me out, and Breedie's father said nothing; he stayed sitting, his hands clasped before him, like a judge listening and weighing evidence. I walked across the gravel at the front of their house towards their avenue, and just as I reached the part of the avenue where the bend of it and the position of the trees hide you as you walk from the road and the house I heard the breath of him behind me, and before I had time to turn, he pushed me, and I fell.

I turned on the ground and looked up at him, and a light burnt in his eyes and the whites of them were shot with zigzags of blood I hadn't noticed in the house, and I was propped up on my elbows now, and he dropped down to a kneel and I screamed without sound, and he was straddling me so I couldn't move backwards or move at all, and there was a salty smell off him and a vague stale aftershave smell, and he took a fistful of my hair in one hand and put his other hand around my face and squeezed hard so my lips were puckered forward, and his teeth when he spoke seemed small and sharp, and in a quiet, slow and even voice he said, You little bitch. I know what you did. You and your gang of fucking sluts. You know nothing about the world. But I know all about you. And he pushed me back onto the stones and he got up and turned away from me and walked back towards his house. And I ran the road home with a feeling of a presence behind me, salty-smelling and dark, and I lay on my bed for hours that day, and told my father I was feeling sick, to go away, he couldn't help me, and I rang Pat that night and told him to meet me at the handball alley, and I let him do what he'd wanted to do that whole year, what he'd begged me to let him do, up against the cold wall with my skirt hitched up around my waist, and I held to him tight and thought about the dark and searing thing in Breedie Flynn's father's eyes.

The heat of these cloudless days is starting to get to me now. I sit for hours and sweat, and Daddy laughs and says I'd be as well off out in it, going for a walk or something, or sitting in the shade beneath the maples at least, enjoying it while it lasts. We always get a blast around now, he says, a taster of what we could have had all along if we weren't in a place so disposed to rain, and we always fall for it and think we're in for a smashing second half to the summer, and we're disappointed as a rule. It's only a tease, he says, but we have a right to allow ourselves to be teased. Still he went to town and bought an electric fan, and set it up in front of me, and he made me put my bare feet on a pouffe, and he brought me

Diet Coke with ice in it, and the coldness and the caffeine made the baby jerk and kick.

He drove me every day last week to Limerick to see Mary Crothery, and every day she'd brightened a bit more. The only deep slash was below her left shoulder, so the surgeons had to clip and stitch the muscle tissue back together, and that's the sorest part, she says. There are lines of stitches down along her face and arm and leg, like foul crawling creatures, and a rose-shaped bruise of purplish black on her right cheek, and I kissed her there without thinking and she flinched. But there's a feeling about her of peace, almost of joy, and she's more beautiful now than she ever was before, even with her bruises and the slashes on her flesh. With her hair down loose about her face and her bright white shift and the soft light that settles on her from the high window, where someone placed a statue of Our Lady to watch over her, she looks like a wingless angel, tiny and delicate, propped on pillows in her hospital bed. She said to me: I seen Heaven, miss, and I won't never be afraid of death again.

That girl can't go back to the halting site, Daddy said, as we drove home from Limerick today. We'd met Mary's mother at the hospital door and she'd stuck in me, saying, I hadn't much to be doing to say I could give all my days to visiting hospitals, and her husband wouldn't be able to stand on his two legs maybe ever again but there was no one worried one bit about that, only all above gawking in at *that wan!* And why was I so worried anyway? My father stepped between us and Mommy Crothery softened a bit when she saw him and she jabbed her John Player out on a sign that said NO SMOKING IN HOSPITAL GROUNDS and said, Good day to you, sir, I don't know you, and I'm sorry now for giving out in front of you but these is terrible times for my family, as you may know, and all about us is enemies and hard people who would do for us without blinking, and it's the way things is gone now that we don't know friend from foe. And them boys is no use, she said loudly, gesturing at the file of bowl-cut foot soldiers from the blurred place before manhood, standing sentry still for fear the Folans, or whomever of their cohort had carried out the attack, would come back to take a Crothery, or a cousin of a Crothery, all the way to Heaven or to Hell. And them out there is worse again, Mommy said, sweeping her eyes and her arm out farther to the standing squad car at the side of the hospital gate, watching all comers and goers and glancing uneasily now and again at the shuffling shamefaced sentinels strung across the hospital entrance.

There's no law among those people, only their own, Daddy said, as he drove. There's no let-up once a thing like that starts, and wrong after wrong will be done in the name of putting right some initial wrong known only to them. He looked across at me and his face was pale and he was gripping the gearstick tight. When it comes to fighting and honour and feuds and all that bloody stuff there can be no reasoning with them. I knew many's the tinker along the years. We'd meet them often on the sides of roads when I was on the council crews. Many of them were as decent as the day is long. But they'd swipe all before them, all the same and think nothing of it. They used to often circle us when we were doing big jobs, like vultures above a dying animal, watching machinery and tanks of diesel and trailers and bales of wire and all sorts of plant. And we came to know the way they see the world, just by the odd conversation we'd have here and there with them. The small things they'd drop into a conversation. You could see the steel inside in them when it came to certain things. Daddy lowered his voice. Look. You could bate a Traveller all day long. You could saw off his arms. He'll stay coming at you till there's one of you dead.

And I had no reply for him, and no energy to argue, and I

thought of Martin Toppy's gentle voice as he read his Dr Seuss aloud, and his eyes as he looked up at me to ask had I ever ate green eggs and ham, and was there such a thing at all. And I thought of Martin Toppy's lips on mine, the heat of them, and the terrible wrong I'd done that boy, to add to all the other wrongs I've done.

So the way I said it happened is still true. A sudden bursting out and letting go, as uncontrolled and uncontrollable as a wasp-stung mastiff or a charging unbroken colt or a dam burst or a lightning strike, a thing blindly and dumbly intent on its own happening and course and conclusion. Martin Toppy had no choice but to put his lips on mine that day, and his work-hardened hands on me, and I could lie and say it was a sudden thing, a terrible momentary weakness, an overcoming; but I planned it, I wanted it, I knew exactly what I was doing, and I ignored myself, the shrill, beseeching voice inside my head, saying, Melody, Melody, what the fuck are you doing? Why the fuck are you trying to seduce that boy? And when he'd finished saying he loved me and promising to kill for me and he had left at last, I lay flat and raised my legs and rested my feet against the wall, so none of him would be wasted, to maximize my chances. I did that, imagine, and if you held a gun against my head and asked me why, I couldn't tell you.

Week Thirty-five

THE FATNESS OF me suddenly, all swollen and puckered and filled. Daddy gives me sausages and rashers and fried eggs and white toast buttered thick and coffee with sugar and cream in the mornings, and chops or steaks or chicken roasted in its crackling skin and draped with bacon, with spuds and gravy and vegetables mashed to a buttery salty paste in the evenings, and he makes me graze all day on sandwiches, daintily cut and filled with dangerous delicious things, and slices of slathered fruitcake. Mary Crothery watches wide-eyed, picking like a sparrow, and says, Lord save us, miss. You're the size of a house. You'll have Ireland ate before this babby is out.

And my father laughs at all her proclamations and says, Mary, you're a card.

I stood today in the kitchen, watching out the window from the sink. Daddy was standing facing the hedge at the bottom of

the garden where the maples and the elderberry meet, and he was
gesturing, making little pictures with his hands. It seemed as
though he was talking to himself, or to someone who was hidden
in the greenery, but then I saw Mary, sitting on the bench behind
him, half hidden by the last in the row of apple trees that bisects
the garden, and she was facing back, looking at him while he
talked, with one leg tucked beneath her, her arms crossed on the
top board of the bench-back, her chin resting on them. Now and
then she seemed to laugh, or to shake her head in wonder. And I
knew that Daddy was explaining something about the wildlife of
the hedgerow, or the flowers or the plants, and I imagined myself
in Mary's place, bored and impatient, willing him to stop. And I
felt a little bolt of pain, a singeing moment of regret. And then
they both were silent, and Mary's chin was raised now from her
arms, and they were watching a spot beside the trunk of the maple
tree, and they were perfectly still, and after a long moment, a
minute or so, my father turned slowly around to her and he was
smiling, and Mary had one hand across her mouth, and her eyes
were opened wide.

They walked together back along the gentle slope to the
house, and they seemed so easy in each other's company I half
expected her to link his arm, but I knew she never would: it's not
a thing that she would ever do. I know this for a fact and yet
I don't know how or why I know. They came into the kitchen
carrying cut grass on their shoes and I gave out to them, and
Daddy rolled his eyes and sighed and shook his head in mock
censure, and Mary laughed at his little act, and toed her heels to
slip her runners off, and stood there in her stonewashed jeans and
her pink hoodie and her bare feet with her toenails painted red,
and Daddy stood behind her saying, Ah, boys, ah, boys, we had a
good look at the bees, hadn't we, Mary? And Mary's eyes were
shining and brimming with some excitement, something she had

to say to me that she'd learnt just moments ago, to see if I knew this wondrous thing that she now knew. And the sky and the earth and the cut grass and the chirruping of birds and the low drone of insects and the slant of light across my father's happy face and the gleam of wonder in Mary Crothery's eyes and the smell of the morning air and the weight of life inside me all seemed even, and easy, and massless, and perfect, and right, and every deficit seemed closed in that moment.

The bees dance, Mary Crothery said. Lord almighty, I seen it with my own eyes, otherwise I wouldn't have believed it. Your father showed me it, the dance they do right there in mid-air, to tell their friends where to go for to get the pollen. They wag their little legs around in circles and they kick in and out the very same as people doing Irish dancing or ballet or one of them, and their little bodies hop and jig around in the air, and their friends all sit in the air around them, what is it, oh, ya, *hovering*, and watches them, and that's the way the dancing bee gives directions to the others, and the place where all the pollen is could be miles away, and he'll tell them down to the last inch whereabouts the flowers are, and how much pollen have they, and what type of flowers they are in the field and all, and once the dance is done the watchers all fly off, and the dancer has a rest and goes again, to find more places where there's pollen waiting.

Mary sat and poured a drop of tea for Daddy, and asked him was it drawn enough for him, and he said it was, and so she poured again and filled his mug. And then she poured for me and her, and she shook her head again, and lowered her voice, and asked me did I think my father was pulling her leg. Could that really be true? And I told her it was, I'd heard it before, and Daddy laughed and said, Lord God, if I was that good at making up things I'd be a rich man.

Well, what about the one about the bumblebees? Mary asked, and Daddy made a face pretending offence, and Mary said he'd told her nobody knew how it was bumblebees was able to fly; there's no one knows what gets their big fat bodies off of the ground. Their wings is woeful small, too small to carry all that weight into the air; the way they fly is, what's it again?

And Daddy said, A scientific impossibility.

Oh, ya. Imagine that. A scientific impossibility. Doesn't that just show you, though? And we both looked at Mary Crothery, who was smiling through a wispy cloud of steam, and there was a kind of serenity about her, a happy satisfaction at her haul of mysteries, the dance of the worker bees and the mystery of the bumble's flight, and she said: Doesn't that just show you the power of God?

And Daddy said, It does, it does surely, and I smiled and said, There's a pair of ye in it, and Mary Crothery laughed, and the dark slash along her face seemed not as livid in the morning sun.

Mary's parents and her sisters and brother and their relatives from the site at the Ashdown Road came today to Daddy's house, and stopped on the grass along by the outside of the front wall, a Transit van and a mobile home behind it, and a car behind that and a trailer and another car again with a wagon behind, and more vans and cars and wagons strung along the roadside, outside the houses and the farms of the Comerfords, and the Brien Cutters, and the Gleesons, and I can imagine the terror those neighbours felt, at this apocalypse of nomads at their gates.

Mary Crothery's mother stepped alone through my father's gate and in along the gravel yard, and he and I and Mary went to meet her. She stopped beside a bush of yellow roses and we stopped too, and Mary's wounded father sat bedraggled and dark-eyed and downcast, watching through the closed window of his van's passenger side, and Mommy stood in silence a long while, an arm's length from us, regarding us without expression, her bare arms hanging, the copious flesh of them reddened from the sun, her yellow hair wound tight atop her head.

Would you not think of tarmacking that, sir? And she pointed to the ground around her feet, and my father said, no, he'd sooner gravel any day. At least it never melted in the sun. And Mommy told him gravel wasn't worth a curse, and her husband and his crew done tar that thick, and she stretched her thumb and fore-finger to their limits to signify the thickness of her family's tar. Someday, please God, we'll lay tar there for you in thanks. And anyway that isn't why I come, she said, and she laid her eyes on Mary, standing silent beside me, and she said, Come here to me, daughter, and Mary walked towards her, and Mommy took her in her arms and hugged her to her massive chest, and Mary put her arms around the girth of her mother and they stood there cheek to cheek in that embrace awhile.

We witnessed this from where we stood, and Mary's kith and kin and clan watched on from all the waiting wagons on the road, their engines ticking over and their exhausts breathing blue plumes into the clean air, and Mommy after long moments held Mary out away from her, her hands on both her upper arms, and said, We have to leave you here, and take ourselves away up to the north of Ireland, the way we'll get protection from them that has the power to give it. And your father and your uncles will come back once things is organized, and there'll be a fair fight fought between two men and two men only, and all these fires will be quenched with the help of God. And I'm sorry for what happened you, daughter, and I hope you can forgive the cold way I was with you, and the next time we lay eyes on one another this trouble will all be done with.

And Mary Crothery's mother plucked from among her necklaces a thin chain of gold with a crucifix on it, and she laid it on her daughter and she fastened it at Mary's nape, and the cross sat in the hollow below Mary's throat and she fingered it with reverence and said, Oh, Mommy. There's no forgiveness needed. Not between me and you, not ever. And Mary Crothery stood, head bowed, and put one hand across her heart and one hand across her eyes, and her mother walked around her to where we stood, Daddy and I, and she thanked my father for the sanctuary and safety he had offered to her daughter, and she shook his hand, and she shook my hand but never met my eyes, and as she passed back she put an envelope into Mary's hand and said, Child, you're to give that to that man. That's to keep you.

And before my father could protest she was gone, and she had swung back into the driver's seat beside her diminished husband, and she had delivered Mary's final punishment, this leaving of her, and the motorcade rolled slowly away, and it stopped again not ten seconds up the road, and two shapes climbed from the back of a car, one small and one not much bigger, and they ran back along the verge and in our gate, and it was Margaret and Bridget, and they were sandalled and bare-legged in matching pairs of scanty denim cut-offs, and belly-tops of whitest white, and they were spangled in bracelets and rings, and they wrapped their arms around their older sister and they wailed all three. And a horn blew and they ran back the way they'd come and Mary Crothery's family clattered away, away from her, in a haze of dust and diesel fumes.

Week Thirty-six

THE SUN IS stubborn now and won't give ground to rain. Each morning's haze is burnt away by noon and all the earth is cracked and baked, and all the grass is brown and yellow, scorched to temporary death. The farmers must be praying for a drop, Daddy says, and checks about for prying eyes while he defies the hosepipe ban to slake his flowers' thirst. They'll want to do another cut and there's no growth. Mary Crothery sits in silence beside me on the patio beneath the shade of the parasol that skewers the picnic table, and she caresses the cross below her throat, and she toes the dust on the flagstones and she swats away the flies with hissed curses, and she asks me over and over am I okay, do I want anything, and once, a few days ago, I snapped at her that I was fine, I was fine, leave me alone, will you, and I didn't feel my temper rising till the words were out, and she said, Go way and fuck off so, you cow, and her eyes filled with tears and I tried to make it seem as though I was joking, and she said, This heat would wear an angel's temper, and I said, I'm no angel, that's for sure, and she looked at me and said, You are, miss, that's just exactly what you are. You and your father. Two angels that rescued me.

Mary Crothery has a phone again and she asks for help with texts. I don't know who she could be texting. Margaret and Bridget, I suppose. Or some cousins, now her quarantine is lifted, and her sins have been expunged by blood. Spell bollocks, miss. B-O-L-O-X, is it? That won't go in; the phone keeps changing it. The phone should mind its own business. And she hunches over it and her thumbs work across the screen and the light of it is reflected in her eyes. Mary Crothery calls my father sir. Will you stop calling me sir, he says, and she says, Oh, ya, I forgot, sorry, sir, sorry. And they both laugh.

Travellers are the only true Irish, my father said one day at lunch. Ye never mixed blood with the Vikings nor the English nor the Normans nor any of them. Ye were warriors and chieftains and kings. The Hill of Tara ye came from originally. The royalty of Ireland ye were.

Who were? Mary Crothery said.

Travellers, long ago, my father said. Ye ruled over Ireland and were warriors, and ye fought against every invader that ever took sword against us, and lost all the power and influence ye had for a finish and were set upon the road and never stopped. The very same as the Gypsies abroad in Europe; they're called that because they used to be the rulers of Egypt before the pharaohs even, and were so powerful that they set out to take over other countries, and got repelled at every border so they stayed moving from place to place in search of conquest and for a finish they never stopped.

I always knew that, Mary Crothery said. That's why the country people has no time for us. They're afraid we'll take over again.

Why do you call people who aren't Travellers country people? I asked her.

I don't know in the Hell, she said, and raised her cross to her lips at the mention of that foul place, to rid her lips of the sin of the saying of it, and to protect herself from its clutches.

Pat drove into Daddy's yard today. He met us at the halfway point between the gate and house, Mary and me, just walking out to see could we find the Comerfords' horse, nosing through the bars of their gate. Mary had a bag of knobby unripe apples for him, picked from one of Daddy's trees. Twist them off, Daddy told her, as she picked them, the way they'll grow again next year.

I did, sir, she said, I always does it that way.

And Daddy said, Good girl, good girl, and turned again to his hoeing, whistling and unstiffened, the peak of his cap turned jauntily towards the sky. Two years at least have fallen from his face; his limbs and joints have seemingly unseized. The sun, he says, and the bit of exercise.

The house faces south and so Pat came from out of the sun. I squinted at him and he was stopped beside us before I recognized him. He sat looking up, revving his engine lightly, like a boy racer, his elbow cocked at the window and his other hand lightly resting on the wheel. He could have been eighteen again, if it wasn't for his bald spot and his lines; he could have been driving his mother's car, borrowed for an hour of shifting at the Lookout or the lay-by off the road behind the Height. Hello, he said, and eyed my swollen middle, and Mary Crothery, up and down.

Hello, I said back, and Mary Crothery moved a step away from Pat's car, and in behind me, the way a shy child would when presented to a stranger.

I won't bite you, Pat said.

You wouldn't want to, Mary Crothery said in a low voice,

barely more than a whisper. I'd knock your fuckin teeth out for you.

And Pat's face darkened and he said, What's that, now?

And Mary Crothery said from behind me: Not a thing, sir.

Pat asked me to go for a drive with him and I said, No.

Mary Crothery continued towards the gate, saying, I'll leave you at it, miss. I'll go down and say hello to the horse. If you scream I'll hear you.

Pat curled his lip as he watched her walk away in his wing mirror and said, She's a fuckin bould yoke, isn't she? Then he looked up at me and said, Come on. Please, Mel.

It's a long time since he last called me Mel. It's a long time since he drove into my father's yard. It's a long time since I wanted to go with him, and have him press his lips against my skin, and squeeze my hand against his chest so I could feel his pounding heart, and hear him say, Do you feel the way it's pounding, Mel, do you feel it? That's what you do to me. You make my heart beat out of my chest. It's a long time since the time before the festering, the regime of nicks and cuts, the terrible and savage war of attrition that I ended with my neutron bomb of happy news.

Come on, Mel, please, Pat said again, and suddenly I was walking around to the passenger side, and he was drumming his thumbs on the steering wheel, and he was leaning forward and smiling, adjusting himself for the spin, and he had a devilish look on his face that used to always weaken me, and make me have to remind myself to be strong and to not give in to him, to not be melted by the heat between us, to stay good. And I never would.

Fuck it, you're after getting quare big, he said, as I got in and he started to reverse out to the road.

Fuck off, I said, and he laughed. And a twist of dust rose up from the roadside ahead, like a mini cyclone in the stillness of the day, and Mary Crothery looked over her shoulder and met my eye as we passed her, and I couldn't read the expression on her face, and Pat and I drove on along the road.

There was a Happy Meal carton squashed on the mat, and a Dinky car and a chewed straw, and I asked Pat what child had been in his car, and he said his nephew, Fidelma's little lad; they'd been home from Canada a few weeks ago. I brought him away over to Kilmastulla, he said, to give a hand drawing silage with the uncle, and he sat up beside me in the tractor and, Lord, he got some kick out of it. He was a pure pleasure so he was, that little man. They're gone back now. He'll be big the next time I see him, I bet you. I'll probably never see him as a child again, imagine. Only on Skype, maybe. You can't draw silage on Skype, though, that's for sure and certain. And Pat put on his sunglasses to try to hide his tears from me.

And all the words I had for him were Oh, Pat, and even they suffered death as they crossed my lips.

Fidelma was going to call out to you, he said, after a mile or so of silence, but Mam told her she was on no account to set foot anywhere near you. That one is poison, she said, and this family has no link to her any more. And I sort of panicked when I heard that, Mel. I got a fright to think this might be really it.

There was one other car at the Lookout, parked at an angle from the kerb at the bottom of the long narrow car park. The lake was still and silvery-blue below us; the Clare Hills seemed only the throw of a stone away. Wakes of motor boats were stretched across the water like scrapes on shiny metal. Pat parked halfway down and nudged me as he pulled the handbrake. Watch the two below, he said. In the Clio. Do you remember the girl of the Donnells that was killed out the Limerick Road a few years ago? That's her mother in that car, and the boy driving is the boy that was driving the car that crashed. That boy must think they can't be seen from the road if he parks the car crooked like that. Misfortune. He done time and all. Jaysus, he was a great hurler, too. It's an awful shame. They go off driving together the whole time. The whole place has it they're doing a line. He calls out to Ballinaclough Cross to pick her up. I think they think they're doing a great job of staying on the QT but every fucker has them well clocked. And she having a husband at home, and he the boy that killed her daughter. Imagine that. The husband fell hard into the drink, though, by all accounts. And Pat shook his head in censorious resignation, and he breathed in deeply and looked at me, and smiled, and said, Ah, sure. What about it? It takes all sorts. We can't judge anyone anyway, me or you. Can we? And it hit me fully then just where I was, the ludicrousness of the situation I was in, sitting in a car with Pat, at the Lookout, where teenagers come to shift, where we used to come to shift, and boy racers come to make circles of rubber on the tarmac, and tourists stop to look at the greenness of the mountains and the blueness of the lake, or, more often, the misting rain and the ghostly hulking shapes behind it, the infinite variations of grey.

And I nearly let him kiss me, imagine. And worse again is I've felt a kind of regret rising unbidden from inside me these last few days since we went for our drive that I didn't let him kiss me. Can't we call it quits, he said, and start again from zero? Can't we call the books balanced and close them and throw them all away and forget about them? Look it. I done the dirt with the prostitutes. You done the dirt with the internet cunt. You got caught out, fair enough. That could happen anyone. I'll get my works put back together and we'll try and try again. A little brother or sister for . . . And he hadn't a word for what was inside me, to put a name on this alien life. They have great strides made now, you know. Your man told me that inside in the clinic the time I went in. I went private so he was mad for chat. An Arab he was, of course. I'd say he charged me an extra bit for every word out of his mouth. Lasers, they use now, and micro yokes and all that stuff. They could undo what they done as quick as they done it. I could be firing live rounds again by next week. Jesus, your tits are gone massive.

And he stretched his arm across and I thought he was going for my breasts, and I slapped his hand hard downwards, and said, Jesus, Pat, and he looked hurt at me and said, No, fuck's sake, Melody, I only wanted to put my hand *there* a second. And he looked down and slowly laid his hand across my stomach, and he left it resting gently there, and the warmth of it soaked into me, to us. I only wanted to see what it would feel like, Pat said in a whisper, and he sat and looked across at the Clare Hills and so did I and we were silent for a while, and all the years of wounding seemed in those moments to fade, and to lose their form and realness, like an ungraspable dream, dissolving in the moments after waking. And a summer breeze rolled down along the slope of the hills and out across the water and made ripples there that danced for a second with the light and then were gone.

Imagine my mother's face, Pat said, as he drove me home, if I arrived on with you now. It was probably she put the brick through your window, you know. Hey. Will we go for one spin down through the village, for the gallery? Just so everyone knows we're on good terms? So smartarses know to watch their fuckin jaws?

And I said, No, and he said that was fair enough, and he drew his car along by Daddy's outside wall and stopped there. I won't drive in, he said. And I don't know how it took me so long to figure this out, but I saw then, maybe because we were out of the sun's glare, in the shade of the willow that sentries the lawn, the slight dilation of his pupils, and the shrill light in his irises, and the slight yellowness of the sclera of his eyes, and the mad weave of bloody lines at their edges. I said, Pat, are you on something?

And he looked at me in silence and he opened his mouth, and there was a lie on his lips, I knew, and he seemed to think better of the lie and so he closed his mouth again and he looked away from me and he said nothing for a minute, then he whispered: Yokes the doctor gave me. My nerves came at me a bit. I couldn't sleep or eat for a good long while. I took my father's gun one day and walked along the river path down towards Ballyartella and the time got away on me and when they saw the gun gone and me gone too they panicked and my father ran the whole way down and when he met me at the end of Stack's Lane at the bend of the river he could hardly breathe and I had the gun loaded but I was only hoping for a shot at a duck, that's all, but my father took the gun off of me and he took the cartridges out and fucked them into the river and he started crying and saying, Jesus, son, Jesus, son, there's no woman worth that, and it gave me an awful hop to see him that upset and so I went to the doctor to please him, really. To please them all. The way they wouldn't be worrying about me and fucking mithering non-stop.

I thought of Paddy and his envelope of cash, and his plans for my exile. All fathers are the same in extremes, all parents. They'll do anything they can to save their young from pain.

My father met me at the door and he said, Well? How's the boy? The boy, he always called Pat. I'd forgotten that. He hasn't called him that in years. I know how fond he always was of Pat; he never could disguise it. They often stood together at the school wall to watch a match in the hurling field. I wouldn't please the fuckers hand over a fiver to go into an underage match, Daddy would say, and Pat would agree, and they'd both come home half blind from squinting across the distance to the field and they'd often be sunburnt from standing in the open when they could have sat in the cool shade of the stand. They footed turf together in

Cloughjordan bog and bagged it and drew it home on a borrowed trailer and divided it equally between our houses. They each agreed with everything the other said on hurling, and cars, and politics, and which fella was stone useless and which fella would be the saving of us all, and it was hard sometimes to figure out what they were talking about, but they always seemed relaxed together, and words flowed back and forth between them easily. Pat is a man that's liked by men and so is my father.

He's fine, Dad, I said. There's no fear of him.

And how's his parents, and the girl, Fidelma? Did she have a child, ever?

And I said she did, a little boy, remember? They went to Canada shortly after he was born?

And Dad inspected the ceiling as though scanning the whiteness there for some clue as to the whereabouts of the memories of these things, and he said, Oh, yes, of course, I have it now. And how is she getting on over there?

And I lost my temper then, suddenly, with no sign given to me beforehand of its imminent departure, and I shouted, Jesus Christ, Dad, for fuck's sake, how the fuck would I know how she is? Do you think she fucking rings me and tells me or writes to me or something? That family think I'm shit, Dad, and they always did. And I stood fuming, waiting for the cooling, breathing deeply in and out.

And my father took his glasses off and wiped them on his sleeve and said, I was only asking, the way anyone would. Go easy now, lovey, don't be vexed. Please don't be vexed, now. Come in and sit down and I'll make you a bit to eat.

Week Thirty-seven

MARY CROTHERY HAS been sour with me the last few days. She won't sit across from me at meals the way she always does, but takes the place at the far end of the table, facing Daddy, as far from me as she can get. She won't meet my eye. Even going through her word cards and our stack of Dr Seusses she hasn't once laughed, and her reading is mechanical and clipped. When stuck on a word she stays silent and downcast; instead of laughing or rolling her eyes heavenward she looks sullenly at the page and purses her lips. Today I felt my patience stretching to its last. I tried to push away my rising anger, to keep my temper even. Mary, love, I said, why are you so cross with me?

I'm not one bit cross, miss. Not one bit.

Why won't you talk to me, then?

Amn't I talking now? What more do you want from me?

I want to know what happened to make you so cross with me.

The way you drove past me the other day, she said, and she

stopped and bit her lower lip and I felt a burning in my stomach
and the echo of a distant pain behind my heart. With your
husband. The very same as if I wasn't there. The very same as if I
was a stranger. But I have no right in the whole wide world to be
one bit cross over that. And you're still married to that man and
he has his rights as well. I just never thought in a millen years
you'd turn away from me so fast. We was going for our walk to see
the horse and the day was so lovely and I was so happy and the
very minute *he* arrived you was gone from me, and I seen the look
he gave me driving past, and the look you gave me wasn't far
behind. And Mary squeezed her eyes tight shut and put her hand
across her mouth when she saw me start to cry, and she put her
other hand out and squeezed my wrist, and from behind her hand
she said, Oh, miss, I don't know what come over me. I don't know
why I got so wicked. And you so good to me always. I think it's just
the way I was so jealous when I seen you driving off for a spin
in the car with your husband. What I wouldn't have gave for it to
of been Buzzy drove in the gate, and brang me off to try and woo
me back.

The weather broke today. It shook and bellowed and lightning
sheeted across the sky as a low pressure front came crashing in
from the ocean like a barbarous horde and slew the tyrannous
high. Daddy and Mary and I stood close together and looked
up at the sky from the patio door like people seeing the aurora
borealis for the first time, like people not used to rain. There
was a sharp metallic smell in the air and the soil blackened
and turned to mud beneath the pounding rain and the flowers
cowered in their beds and the branches of trees waved in the
sudden wind as if rejoicing. Mary Crothery counted aloud
the seconds between flashes and peals, and blessed herself at
every rolling boom. She held her hand out from the doorway to

feel the giant drops. The world will be washed away, she said.

The rain has stopped falling now and has started its journey skyward again in ghostly wisps. Mary asked me this evening, as I sat in the soaked garden sweating in the cloying air, if I still thought Pat was any way good-looking. I said I'd never really found him unattractive, it was just that we were so wrapped in one another for so long it was as though we stopped seeing one another as separate people, so being hard on each other became like being hard on ourselves: when I was really unhappy with myself I told him I hated him; I blamed him for things that weren't his fault.

What kinds of things? Mary Crothery wanted to know.

All kinds, I told her. A cracked glass. A late taxi. A rainy day. A dead baby.

She said, Oh, Lord, miss, you guv him hell.

I said, I did, and he was well able to give it right back.

Mary said, Traveller girls marry young as a rule. Most keeps their mouths shut, though. I seen women getting thrown around the place, bate black and blue. I seen more girls and women stone mad for their men, though, acting like they were gods. I seen a woman one time whose man was killed in a car crash lay herself along the mound of his grave and it took seven or eight people a good few hours to move her off of it. And still she went back every day and lay down alongside that mound of earth and for all I know she's still doing it. She was a cousin of Buzzy's through marriage. He was real good to her at the time. Helped her out no end. Buzzy never seen no one stuck.

His family nearly killed you, Mary, I said, and she turned her head sharply away from me and looked affronted, insulted almost by the existence of this truth.

He'd of had nothing to do with that. Buzzy knew I done what I had to do. Buzzy knew me. That's all over other things.

Tarmacaddanin and roofing and all that. Rackets all the men do be at. I was only an excuse to be fighting. Buzzy had a great heart underneath.

Underneath what? I asked her.

You know. All the oul shaping men must do. All the oul walking around like peacocks.

I went to Portiuncula again today, on my own. I left when Dad was gone to Mass and Mary had her physiotherapy appointment. I dropped her at the clinic and asked was she okay to walk back home. The sky was a lighter grey, tinged with sickly yellow, and seemed wrung out, but still there was a hint of wetness in the breeze. There's fear of me, she said, and that's a fact. There's no one going to touch me on the street. Our enemies are all far away. I feel that in my bones and in my heart. It's the way I have a taste of the vision, don't forget. And she smiled at me and pulled her hood up over her head. I hadn't thought of violence, only rain.

The nurse smiled at me, the same one as last time, warmer now, it seemed. The size of me, maybe, the nearness of the end, or the beginning. But I haven't prepared for a beginning, only for an end. Does she know this? The ultrasound technician held my eye while she smoothed the gel onto my bare distended skin and smiled as well, and there was some kind of light of knowing in her eyes, some ghost of wryness in the upturn of her lips. I wonder if she somehow knows my secret too. I feel no worry. What if she does? What if they all do? It doesn't seem to matter. These people know their jobs and anything else they know doesn't matter. The baby's heartbeat pounded through the amplifier, and I asked the girl was it meant to be so fast.

Oh, yes, she said, and she flicked a strand of blonde hair that had escaped her ponytail back from her face. It's completely normal. Look, it's like he's waving, or dancing even, the way his legs are going! And she put a hand on my forearm and squeezed lightly while we watched my baby raise his arms and lower them in turn, and straighten out the slope of his back and settle again into a curve, and kick first one leg up and then the other. Here was the product of my madness, the corporeal evidence of my degeneration, kicking his legs for me and this pretty girl, whose gloved hand was still lightly on my arm, and we laughed at the little interloper on the screen, and the sunlight shone through the leaves of a tree outside and dappled the white wall behind the machine where my baby danced and danced.

My father was sitting in the kitchen at the table drinking tea when I got home. Is Mary not with you? he said.

No. She had her physiotherapy appointment. For her shoulder and her arm.

Oh, he said. Gor, ye should have let me know and I'd have collected her.

And I didn't know why we hadn't done that. I was so caught up in making sure no one came with me to the hospital. A low pounding began inside me, like my heartbeat was being amplified by the same machine that had amplified my baby's, but only in my ears, and my brain sensed panic and dumbly dumped a barrow of adrenalin into my stomach in case I needed to run, to flee something, or to fight.

I'm surprised at you, Melody, my father said, letting her off around the town on her own. There could be anyone lying in wait for her. They could be back to finish the job.

I said, Jesus, Dad, you go look for her then, drive down to the clinic and around the town, and he whitened suddenly and stood so fast his chair flew back and he banged against the table so his mug shook and tea slopped out of it and he was gone past me, and

I was behind him saying, Wait, Dad, wait for me, I'll go with you.

We found her on the Ashdown Road, halfway down the far side of the Long Hill, a half-mile from the halting site that used to be her home. She was walking slowly with her hood pulled up still despite the heat, and her shoulders were hunched as though she was trying to make herself smaller, to hide herself. Daddy drew along beside her and drove at her walking pace and I lowered my window and said, Mary, and I said it again, and she kept walking and didn't turn her head, and I shouted this time, MARY!

And at last she turned, and seemed shocked to see us there, like kerb-crawlers looking to do business, and she said, What? I'm only going for a look.

A look at what?

Daddy was leaning out over his steering wheel and he was saying, Come on, sweetheart, and we'll give you a spin. Is it down to the site you're going?

And Mary stopped walking and said, Go way, will ye, and leave me be. I'm only going for a look to see who's there and I'll be back in a little while. Go on, she said, louder now, I'm grand now, I'm the finest evermore.

The finest evermore, she said. She got that from my father. It sounded lovely from her lips, like some sweet tribute to him. A part of me is jealous she's so cracked about my father, and all of me is jealous he's so cracked in return. But I can't begrudge her.

Mary Crothery had met someone from the depleted halting site at the waiting room in the hospital, a distant cousin, sufficiently far out to not have had to flee with all the rest. The bays left empty by the exodus of Crotherys and Toppys were being filled by new people, some of whom had never before set foot in Ireland. And still they went around calling themselves Irish, Mary said.

And the English accents of them, you wouldn't believe. You could hardly make out one thing they were saying. Some of the Toppys were back as well, the distant cousin said, and everyone was glad of that because Mick Toppy'd keep them all in line, they knew, and no fight could be fought in his presence that wasn't directed by him or that wasn't involving him, but still and all everything was tense and dark about the place, and the small boys even weren't inclined to play outside, but stayed inside their wagons, peeping out.

Mary Crothery stood in the kitchen and told us all this, and the sun was setting behind her and reddening the sky above Ton Tenna, and the crows were processing home in a straggled weary line, and she looked at me and said: It's Martin Toppy's going fighting for us, miss. The boy you know whose book you gave me to mind. And my hands went of their own accord and joined themselves across my womb and Mary Crothery's eyes followed them down, and a light of knowing flashed there for a moment and was gone, and the hard and heavy silence was softened by my father saying gently, Ah, boys, ah, boys.

Mick Toppy has claim to be king of all Travellers, you know. His father is buried beyond in Loughrea in County Galway and it says on his gravestone: Here Lies Michael Toppy the King of All Travellers. I seen it with my own two eyes the time we buried an aunt of Mommy's up there. There was a line of people waiting to pay tribute at his grave, and he years dead at this stage, and to kiss the head-stone and all. There was women bowing before the dead man, and children crying that never once laid eyes on him. The thought the Travellers had a king one time that now was dead was enough sadness to bring their tears. Anyway, anyhow, that's what it is now and that's what it's going to be. The grandson of a king is going fighting for us, and no one knows yet who the Folans will send.

And Mary laid her hands palms upwards on her knees and she folded herself forward and laid her forehead on her palms, and a keening wail came from her, and my father stood from his garden chair and said, Ah, now, ah, now, and Mary straightened herself and looked at us through eyes half blind from tears and said, What will I do? What will I do if it's Buzzy they send?

Week Thirty-eight

MORE ROLLED IN overnight, vans and wagons full of dark-faced men and brass-blonde women. They filled the space at the front end of the site that Mary's family had left empty. They parked against the end wall at the back in spaces cleared of scrap and horseboxes on Mary's father's orders, transmitted from their hiding place in the north.

Martin Toppy's regal father welcomes their leaders with over-long handshakes, clasps of arms and touched foreheads. Women step from wagon to wagon without touching the ground; doors are slammed quickly behind them. Children press their faces against nets of brilliant white, laundered for the trip so as not to be a show opposite the Irish people. Curtains stay drawn. Days and nights pass. Still their champion hasn't been seen.

They park close together, leaving gaps just wide enough for a person to walk between each vehicle. As more and more arrive they puddle and thicken; a coagulation of metal and flesh, a dark blockage at the gate of the meadow that rolls up to the site's back wall, where horses graze and a stable was promised once, years ago, by a council candidate who ferried Travellers in and out of town to register and then to vote, and their hundred or so votes swung the day for him, and yet no stable was ever built.

And now they've overflowed the site and started to fill the meadow, and a suited woman with a clipboard held fast to her chest and two luminous-vested men from the council came and remonstrated, and then the guards arrived, and families moved out for show, and returned in darkness, and filled their unofficial berths again. The Folans won't come until the day itself, and no firm day or place for the fight has been agreed. And my baby is hopping inside me, and we've seen the perfect shape of his hand against my skin.

Mary Crothery has been told to stay away from the site in a missive from Mommy relayed through a text from Margaret or Bridget or both of them. We park every day across from the entrance and keep watch, and Daddy hums and twitches with nerves and shifts in his seat and asks us have we not seen enough, and Mary sits low in the back of Daddy's car with her hood up and her hair tied back, peeping, saying, Wan minute, sir, wan minute more, I'm begging you. And all the minutes turn to hours, and it seems they know we're watching, and have tacitly accepted our presence there, as outliers of the tribe, maybe, and Martin Toppy's father has once or twice stood still and looked across, and has met my eye, and nodded, only barely. Oh, Jesus, miss, he seen you, Mary said, and now it's not as scary as it was; there's no one in there not related to Mary, and something of this fight involves her honour, and nothing of it's very clear except the fact of it; it's all boiled down to this slow simmer, the ordered chaos of this coming together, this wait, this nothing-time before the sport. And every day my heart beats harder in my chest whenever Mary Crothery meets my eye. She knows, I know. What she calls her taste of a vision is really a keen intuition, a knowing without conscious thought, a springing to her mind of truths, ushered in there by the tiniest of signals and signs. That she ascribes the provenance of this knowing to a magical force only serves to fasten what she sees as the truth of things harder in her mind; knowledge sent from another realm is incontrovertible, and could not be otherwise. To deny it is to deny God, and the souls of all the faithful departed.

My father wants to go to Jim Gildea and tell him of the coming fight. But he knows that Jim already knows, and so do all the city cops, and there's not one thing that anyone can do, except to hope that the location is sufficiently remote from the rest of the world, and to hope the fair-play family are chosen well, and are sufficiently respected to keep the bout between two men, and the factions from falling on each other, and to hope that no one is killed, and that the fight itself serves its intended purpose, to bring peace, however brittle, however temporary, to this world within a world.

My father fell today at the door of the church. He stumbled on the steps as he left Mass, just as he was blessing himself after dipping his hand in the holy-water font, Minnie Wiley told me, just as she was admiring the straightness of his back, she said, and the nimble way he was walking, like a man who'd received an elixir somewhere, and was reclaiming his youth. Just as she was thinking all of that he fell, and she got a terrible shock when suddenly he was lying there, the very same as if he was dead, and she was sure and certain that he was dead, until she saw him move his legs that were still on the steps and the rest of him on the flags outside the door, and he facing down but his head was sideways, and his arms were out from his sides, like a man who'd tried and failed to fly.

My father had had a stroke. That was what felled him today at the steps of St Mary's. And he had a second stroke as he lay there, his lovely head on someone's folded jacket, Father Cotter praying, having anointed him, and having delivered viaticum just in case. Only a handful or half a dozen maybe would be at a midweek Mass and the circle round my dad was small, and each part of the circle was on its knees, and he was anointed again, and they prayed as they waited for the ambulance to come from Gortlandroe for their brother to be spared, for this not to be his end, because they love my father, all those faithful people, all those holy people we all scorn.

I think about my father bent in prayer on a hard kneeler, his head bowed and his lovely hands together on the pew back in front of him, counting off Hail Marys on his beads, a quick decade after Mass, an offering for me, probably, or for Mary, or for the baby, or for all of us. I wonder if a pain came on him before he fell, if he felt it starting, the dam-burst of blood, if he was scared. I can't bear to think of him feeling scared, saluting his friends and smiling at familiar kneeling people as he left, trying to step it out, to reach the fresh air, to not show his weakening. And yet behind my sadness and my fear for him I feel relief, that he's asleep, and safe here now, and that he mightn't wake until the things I have to do are done.

Mary Crothery's vigil place has changed, to the chair beside my father's bed. He's on a saline drip and a warfarin drip, and there are tubes in his nose that run back along his cheeks and needles piercing his flesh, and his hands are bony and bruised and mottled purple and white and black from the needle tips, and his arms are thin and white, like the hands and arms of an old man, of a man about to die. He's woken now a time or two and turned his head towards us, and there's a bandage on his forehead over his wound from where he fell, and he's tried to speak but he's not able; the workings of his voice are drowned in blood, and the workings of his arms and legs, and the doctors say they'll have to wait until the blood recedes to see what's left, what's possible, what hope there is.

Week Thirty-nine

IT WAS ALL Our Lady's fault but Mary Crothery is having none of that. There's a grotto near the car park where this other, unblemished, Mary stands, her hands out, her head tilted slightly, prettily interrogative, resolutely pinkish-white of face, this Galilean mother, and a mock waterfall runs down a little rockery to her left side, and the water is pumped from a pool at her feet and recirculates eternally. Mary Crothery is not able to pass this place without stopping, and bowing her head, with her arm outstretched so that her hand is beneath the flow of water, and that's what gave them time to make their move; we'd have made it through the gate and out onto the road in the minute Mary offered up in prayer. As it was, a blue van blocked us as we cleared the car-park barricade and its side door slid open and a skinny, dark-faced youth jumped down from it, followed by another and another and the last one armed with a long stout stick, some kind of a bat, and the first one ran across the patch of tarmac separating us and as he did I looked and saw a bollard to my right and a guard box to my left and the barrier closed behind me and no way out for us, no way out, and my right hand moved too slowly to the button that locks all the doors, and Mary Crothery was saying, That's Mav Folan, that's a brother of Buzzy's, and her voice sounded normal, and there was surprise in it, and pleasant wonder, like the voice of a person who has laid eyes unexpectedly on an old friend not met in years, and for all her vision and her second sight she was seeing in that moment no danger, and Mav Folan had his hand on the handle of Mary's door, and I was stabbing at buttons on the centre console of my car and none of them the right one to keep the marauders out, and then the door was open and Mary was being dragged out, and she was screaming at a pitch I've never heard from a human before, and the weapon was swung and it cleared her head because she was falling forward, and one of them had her by her hair and he was pulling her away from me, and the weapon crashed through the glass of the door of my car, and suddenly she was free, and he was reaching for her again, and she had kicked him on his shin to loose his grip, and the open door was blocking them from renewing their arrest, and Mary was somehow back in her seat and I was reversing at the barrier, and I was swinging the car in a mad, screeching arc, and I was finding first, and I was pressing down the pedal to the floor, and as my foot came off the clutch I saw a Traveller boy stand out across our path and I drove straight into him and he dived from our path and from our sight and was gone, and I aimed us at the nose of the blue van and I smashed into it, and there was a great fat man behind the wheel and he was screaming, and his teeth were jagged and yellow and gapped, and his eyes were set wide in his face, and the metal of the nose of his van gave just enough of itself to let us pass, and we bounced up on the kerb and Mary Crothery was thrown forward against the dash and when I looked again she was bloody, and she was moaning at an unearthly pitch, and her nose was at a strange angle in her face.

Martin Toppy appeared today, in the side room of the hospital where Mary was lying broken and bruised once more, the skin of her beautiful face all livid again and coloured with pain, fresh blood tracing the length of the valley of her scar and rusting there to brown. Mary was drugged against her new agonies and was asleep when he came to the doorway, and he stood unmoving there, hulking, half hidden in the shadow of the tiny unlit ante-room that gave into the main room where we were illuminated by shafts of sun through the slats of the blinds. He stooped slightly as he stepped forward from the darkness, and he squinted against the sun. He seemed taller, somehow, and leaner, all the cosseting flesh of his adolescence gone fully now so that his skin was stretched tight over bone and sinew and hard muscle. His face was more sharply angled. He'd become in nine months a man. He looked at me, then at Mary, then back at me. Mary laughed in her sleep, a soft, wry exhalation, knowing, as if she was aware of Martin Toppy's sudden appearance, as if it was the realization of a prophesy, a fortune told to her. The blue of his eyes seemed deeper than before; the light seemed hard and sharp in them. He spoke in a low and even whisper.

Is that a child of mine you're carrying?

I shook my head and told him no, it was my husband's, and my lie hung there in the antiseptic air, and he seemed to examine it, and to accept my words, and to know the untruth of them. And the dust motes glinted and danced in the streaming light, and we watched them in silence awhile, for what was there to be said? And he nodded, and then he looked again at Mary, more closely this time, at the bruises and the cuts on her face, the gash on her cheek from the last assault, her bee-stung lips, her broken nose.

He stayed still but his face changed. His hands were by his sides and balled to fists. A chill seemed to enter the air about him, the light to fade from the room, as though the sun itself was fearful of the trouble to come, and had seen enough already, and wanted nothing more to do with it.

Mary Crothery woke and looked at him for silent moments and said, Hello, dear cousin.

And Martin Toppy straightened himself and lifted his chin and regarded her coldly, but his coldness wasn't towards her. Was it Mav Folan done that to you? His voice was still even but louder now, and there was a brittleness in it, as though it could fracture and crack and become shards, as though his words could any moment break to cries. And Mary whispered that it wasn't. It was that wan's stupid driving done the damage. And she pointed at me and laughed. But they was trying to take me, that's the truth. I don't know for why or for what.

They broke the agreement that was made. This was to be ended the proper way. Them people don't know reason. There'll be no rest for you, Mary Crothery, while them Folans have a grievance against your people, Martin Toppy said. And there'll be no rest for me until this is over and done with. And that's it.

That's it, he said, a coda often tacked to Traveller speech, a circumscription used to close off contradiction or argument or further enquiry. So that was final, that was the way of things, and Martin Toppy had said to us all he would say or need to say.

And before Mary Crothery could form a word of answer or warning or thanks to him, he had turned from us and was gone, and only coldness was left in the space where he had stood.

Week Forty

SOMEONE HIT JUNIOR Folan across the back of the head with an iron bar. On a street in Limerick near the back door of a pub where he'd been drinking. The head of the Folan family attacked, and he only barely landed in the town. The Crotherys were blamed, though no one saw it happen. Between that and the attempted taking of Mary, the fair-play family declared the rules breached and the contract defiled: they were going home and would have no more to do with it unless the fair fight was held that very day. The passing of time, it seemed, was making matters worse. Drink was drowning reason and anger was blossoming in the soil of boredom. Junior Folan's hard skull hadn't given way but he'd had to be stitched, and he was meant to stay put in hospital to be observed, but he wouldn't, of course: he discharged himself and marched away from his confinement in a phalanx of hard-faced men, a squad car rolling slowly behind. A sulky race was hastily organized to distract the police, and Martin Toppy and his opponent were taken away in a van by the fair-play family, and some men from each side were allowed to go too, and some neutral parties, and an adolescent hostage from each side was taken to some other secret place, and held as collateral against further unauthorized violence. And the Folans' man, of course, was Buzzy, and when Mary Crothery got the text that told her this she moaned and raised her face to Heaven and asked why, why, why had she to be punished this way.

We're waiting now for word back from the fight. My father opens his eyes every now and then and he seems at times to smile. They're keeping him sedated so his rhythms stay steady and slow and his vessels aren't pressured. If you imagine unconsciousness to be a sea, a smiling young doctor said, your father is standing on a beach, wetting his feet, maybe swimming outwards from the edge now and again, but never too far. And think of the waters in which he swims as healing waters.

Mary Crothery said, Lord, that's a lovely way of putting it, and the doctor smiled at her as he walked back out. And I imagine Daddy there, in his old blue trunks, his face to the sun, tasting salt on a soft breeze and saying, Ah, boys, isn't that lovely, wouldn't that do you the power of good?

Mary's phone keeps lighting and buzzing and never a word of news, just her sisters asking, What's the story, what's the story, what happened? Mary sits in her pyjamas and a dressing-gown I bought for her that she says makes her look like an oul one, and her slippers with puffs of material like rabbits' tails on them, beside my father's bed. She has to stay here one more night, the doctor said. She has to give a statement to the police as well. And she said she will. She'll tell them everything bar the names of who done it. There was not one thing ever fixed for us by police, she says, nor never will be.

*

A calmness has come over me, from where I do not know. I have a pain that's rising and falling away now, and it's getting stronger all the time. I won't keep it secret much longer. It'll start to show on my face as it crosses my middle and starts along my spine. I have to leave my father here, and Mary Crothery, and I have to get to Portiuncula, and I have to let this baby come.

Something happened in the early hours near dawn. A sudden rushing of feet and a distant cacophony, my bed was moving and a tall man with dark eyes was smiling at me and I remembered him from before and my bed was stopped again and I was moving through the air and I landed softly and I was moving up and down; there was a screen that seemed to dissect me, like I was a magician's assistant about to be sawn in half, and there were shadows moving behind it and a needle entered me and the world darkened to black.

There's a person sitting beside my bed in a mask and gown and they're looking intently at me and a gloved hand is holding mine and I'm trying to tell them about the dream I had where a hand holding a silent baby appeared over the magic screen and people were standing with their backs to me and I could hear no baby's cry and I was screaming in my dream, Why is my baby not crying? Why is my baby not crying? and someone turned and moved down towards me and pointed to a table by a window where two gowned people stood with their backs to where I lay, their arms moving in a strange rhythm, and they suddenly stopped, and everything stopped, even time, until the air was rent in two by a long and rising and perfect cry that faded and was replaced by another and another.

*

He didn't tear me on his way into this world, my gentle little man. But the wound across my stomach sears, like a thin stream of boiling water. Colostrum leaks from my breasts and he nuzzles at them open-mouthed, he wails for them, and I cry with him, and he won't take the plastic teat of the bottle and there's anguish in his eyes. I can't let him feed from me. It would make it too hard; I'd surely renege on my covenant if I put him to my breast. My flowing milk would drown my resolve. He was lifted gently from the dark inside of me into the light, his fists clenched tight, with a tuft of black hair on his head. He was massaged and slapped, cajoled into his first breath. I woke and he was suddenly there and his eyes were blue, like his father's, and full of sadness, it seemed in those first moments.

Shapes pass the frosted window in the door of my room, impressions of people walking in pairs, carrying balloons and bouquets and giant teddy-bears; excited murmurs float along the corridor, smacks of kisses, oohs and ahs. I drift in and out of reality. I wake thinking he's a girl, that I'm in my room at college, that I'm in a hotel with Pat, that I'm home from school with a chest infection, that my mother is sitting beside my bed holding my hand in her cold hand.

His crib is see-through plastic and it's set beside my bed at eye-level and I can lie and watch him as he sleeps and he changes shape with the shifting shadows and the stuttering light; he had wings for a while and he rose a few inches into the air and I screamed and reached for him and my wound scalded and I woke fully and he was sleeping, breathing in and out in perfect rhythm, and I lay back and breathed in time with him and gathered myself, and forced my mind towards reason.

*

A nurse calls now and then to check my wound and heartbeat and antibiotic drip and to see is he feeding, and she asked am I expecting anyone and I said, No, there'll be nobody calling.

And she bit her bottom lip and nodded kindly and looked at me for a few heartbeats and said, Okay, lovey, I'll leave you to it. And they've told me I'm to stay for three more days at least but I can't. I have work to do, things to finish. I have to turn on my phone and make my plans.

He finished his bottle in the end and he's still now, blinking slowly, his eyes fixed on mine. The warmth of him goes into me and through me. Newborn babies can't see well, they say, but my baby can. He can see right into me, now that he's outside of me. All the sounds of the corridor are muted and faraway, and the traffic outside and the lawnmowers and the singing birds; all things orbit us, our perfect mass. My little eight-pound incarnation of perfect goodness, of love, my little god.

Everything that can be known lies behind those eyes. He knows me, all about me, all the terrible things, and he loves me still. I have to hold him to my bare flesh and look at him, and look at him, or it will all have been for nothing. I have to kiss his beautiful cheeks and nose and eyes and ears and head and hold his fingers to my lips and feel the breath of him and breathe him in and take his smell and lock it in my soul. I have to know love of the perfect kind, the kind that exists above all earthly things.

Post-partum

THE WHOLE PLACE is destroyed with dog shit. That's a sentence
my father said today when he woke from a dream. Maybe he was
walking on the riverbank, where people, he always said, seem
to think it's okay to leave their dogs shit away to their heart's con-
tent. He wakes for longer now and he always smiles and sometimes
he speaks, and sometimes he moves his right arm over to his left
and he examines it, and he seems surprised each time afresh by
the stillness and the deadness of it, and then he falls again
back into sleep. Run in there and bring me out the soft wire brush
like a good girl, he said as well, an hour or so after his sudden
complaint about dog shit. Probably to scrape it from the clefts of
the sole of his soiled shoe. Before my mother smells it and loses
her reason. I hope he's finding comfort in his shadow world of
dreams and remembered things and that there are no terrors
lurking there. His face in sleep seems peaceful, anyway. Mary
Crothery left her chain and cross with him; it's fastened round

his neck and Jesus rests in His passion beside my father's heart. If he remembers when he fully wakes and all his veiling mists have cleared he won't feel the loss the way I do, never having seen the baby, or touched him, or smelt his skin or heard his beautiful cry. I couldn't force that sacrifice upon him, after his life of it.

Pat drives over once or twice a week and we drink tea at this kitchen table and sometimes he reaches across for my hand and I let him take it, and hold it while he talks. And I look at the white mark on his ring finger and the flecks of grey in his stubble and the light in his eyes, dancing, the way it always has.

There's no one left now on the Ashdown Road; all the bays are empty and the site is only home to feral cats and rats that skitter and dart about the detritus, and ghosts of people who didn't live here, or die here, but who roam the concrete crannies none-theless. People will come and berth themselves here again, but maybe not this year or next. It will need to be exorcized, cleansed by time, and all the drifting smoke long cleared.

I met them in Portumna, at the entrance to the forest park. Halfway between Portiuncula and home. Martin Toppy and Mary Crothery. Two people barely more than children, but older maybe than I will ever be. Beautiful, the both of them, beyond any words I can find to describe them. Martin Toppy's face was cut and bruised, but it would heal. Mary Crothery was bruised as well, but her scar was fading more each day, doing its best to dis-appear, as though ashamed of its own existence. Martin Toppy had a car, given him by his father. It looked like a good car, safe. A car that might offer protection in a crash, to a baby in a basket in the back, properly strapped and anchored. Martin Toppy had a British driving licence and the car was insured and taxed and tested and cleared by Customs. Martin Toppy was a good driver.

Hadn't he been driving since he could walk? There was no fear there. He could drive like the wind.

The fight had been fair. That was not in doubt. The referees from the fair-play family were there for every blow, hard by in case of dirty digs or boots thrown on the sly, or any breach of the bare-knuckle rules, and it had been decreed and accepted by all that this confluence of the bones and blood and flesh of the matter would be an end to it, and men were there from each of the families to see to this, strung into a jostling ring of shouts and cries and wild exhortations. And the witnesses from outside the feud stood farther back on a bank of grass in silence, and they saw every blow as well, and they had all watched the weary soldiers as they fought, and weakened, and bled, and clung to one another for support, and the accounts that came back to the campsite were from senior men of the assembled tribes and their word could be counted upon as truth. And each man told the same story: that Martin Toppy had stood at the fight's end above Buzzy Folan's unmoving body and howled and screamed his anguish and regret. That a blow of his had killed this man he'd had no quarrel with. That a life had been taken by his hand, and a soul was gone to Heaven years too soon. And that he'd fallen on his knees and begged forgiveness, and that he'd cursed God for allowing him to be born, and that he'd folded himself around Buzzy Folan, and fastened his arms around his neck, and pressed his cheek to his enemy's cheek, and he seemed then to lose all of his reason, for he had cried that he loved him, that he was his brother, and his tears had mingled with the dead man's blood, and their blood and tears had run along the hard ground.

This is what I know, what I've been told. Travellers trust me now, and tell me things. A man from Ennis came to the door a few months ago and stood there with his daughter and his son and he told me he'd heard I was a person who helped Travellers and he asked me would I see what I could do for his children. They hadn't a word of reading between them, he said, and they were gone too old for school. And the world is a harder place now than ever it was before and they can't be left go around ignorant, he said. And more came in the days that followed and I hold classes sometimes now in the hours when Daddy's physiotherapist is here, or the visiting district nurse, or his home help, and I think, when my house is sold and Daddy is stronger and our days have taken up a rhythm, that this is what I'll do with all my days, and I'll do it right and I won't ever fall again to madness. They tell me stories all the time, and I listen, and I don't pretend too much interest for fear they'd get nervous, or suspicious of my interest, and stop.

But nobody knows the whole of my story, nor will I ever tell them. That the name I gave in the hospital on that first visit wasn't mine, nor the PPS number, nor the address. That a person using a false identity had to do so somewhere she wouldn't be known, so I travelled all those miles to Portiuncula to have my baby, instead of in the road to Limerick. That the mother's name on my baby's birth certificate is MARY CROTHERY and that the father's name on my baby's birth certificate is MARTIN TOPPY. That I left my baby in his basket, clipped and strapped and anchored in the back of Martin Toppy's car, and I handed his birth certificate to Mary Crothery, and she could read it, and so could Martin Toppy, and I was proud that they both could read it, because I had taught them, and I had taught them well.

And I told Martin Toppy that this child was his son, and Mary Crothery was its mother, and he didn't meet my eye but he nodded slowly and he looked upon his son's face, and I think some weight was lifted from him. And Mary Crothery held me tight a long time and she pressed her cheek to mine and we anointed one another with our tears.

*

They're gone now, on the road, and they're proper walking people, and they're looking after each other, and they might never come this way again. But I think they will. And maybe they'll find me here, and maybe I'll be happy, and maybe my penance will be done.

Acknowledgements

Thanks:

To Kathryn Court, Victoria Savanh, Christopher C. Smith, and everyone at Penguin Books US; to my editor and friend, Brian Langan, for making me a better writer; to Eoin McHugh, Antony Farrell, Larry Finlay, Bill Scott-Kerr, Fiona Murphy, Ben Willis, Alison Barrow, Sophie Christopher, James Jones, Kate Samano, Hazel Orme, Elspeth Dougall, Brian Walker, Sophie Smyth, Helen Edwards, Ann-Katrin Ziser, and all the people who work so hard to bring my books to the shelves; to the booksellers who ensure they don't linger there; to the readers who make it possible for writers to exist; to Joseph O'Connor and my friends, colleagues and students at the School of Creative Writing and across the University of Limerick; to James Doyle, for his help and advice; to Alan Hayes for his friendship and wisdom; to my wonderful parents, Anne and Donie Ryan, for everything; to Mary, Christopher, Daniel, John, Lindsey, Aoibhinn and all of my family near and far for their love and support; to Anne Marie, Thomas and Lucy, who make it all worthwhile; to the late Mike Finn, Taekwondo Master, gentleman, quiet hero.